I0623708

The Invincible Woman

M.L. Lexi

The last installment of The Determined Woman Series.

Titles by M.L. Lexi

The Blind Woman
The Deceitful Woman
The Forgiving Woman
The Grieving Woman
The Guilty Woman
The Loyal Woman
The Noble Woman
The Resolute Woman
The Unfaithful Woman

The Farfalla Family Saga

The Determined Woman
The Persevering Woman
The Invincible Woman

The Fearless Woman Series

The Fearless Woman
The Naïve Woman

Copyright

"The Invincible Woman" eBook & Paperback Edition Published by M.L. Lexi

All rights reserved. No part of this book may be reproduced or transmitted in any form, or by any means, electronic or mechanical, including photocopying, recording, or by any information storage and retrieval system, without permission in writing from the copyright owner.

This is a work of fiction. Names, characters, places, and incidents either are the product of the author's imagination or are used fictitiously, and any resemblance to any actual persons, living or dead, events, or locales is entirely coincidental.

This eBook/paperback is licensed for your personal enjoyment only. This eBook/paperback may not be re-sold. If you would like to share this book with another person, please do. Thank you for respecting the hard work of this author.

Cover design by M.L. Lexi
ISBN (eBook): 978-1-990660-10-8
ISBN (Paperback): 978-1-990660-11-5
The Invincible Woman Copyright © 2025 by M.L. Lexi
All rights reserved.
Visit our website at www.mllexi.com

For the extraordinary women who shape our world
and inspire us to reach new heights.

Sometimes, it's best to leave the past behind.

—M.L. Lexi

Prologue

REALITY STRUCK AND it all came out.

The betrayal, lying, and plotting that was a part of Antonia Trevi's life like a second skin caused her life to come crashing down like a Jenga tower when the one block that held it together was removed. In a matter of minutes, Antonia—known to her friends as Toni—found herself stripped of everything that had meaning in her life.

Toni had betrayed Bianca, her employer and the only person who believed in her. As a result, Toni lost the job she loved and excelled at. Toni lost the love of the only friends and family she knew. Worse than that, Toni deceived Christian, the only man who gave her unconditional love and expected nothing in return but her love.

Toni's response was to run away, far away from everyone she hurt.

Toni fled to Milan, the only home she knew to welcome her. Putting an ocean between her and the web of lies she concocted was the only plausible conclusion to the situation she created.

Toni couldn't face Christian. It was difficult for Toni to confess her betrayal to Christian's sister, Bianca, but more daunting was revealing to Christian who she truly was. Telling Christian the shameful things Toni did and revealing the humiliation that was her life was something Toni couldn't bring herself to do. The pain of the revelation was all-encompassing, and Toni wouldn't hurt

Christian. Toni wouldn't allow Christian to inherit her trauma.

Absence makes the heart grow fonder, and her absence weighs on him, and he sets off to find her.

When Christian finds Toni, the dam bursts, and she tells him the sordid truth of who she was, what she did, and the lies she had told. With reluctance, Toni revealed she was the type of woman who engaged in relationships with men—many, many men—to extort money from them. Toni told Christian she was a woman who engaged in sexual affairs with older men to satisfy her mother's need for money. Toni conceded she was the type of woman whose questionable past didn't blend with his impeccable upbringing.

Christian held up a silencing hand, but Toni pushed on. "No, Christian. I must tell you everything."

"I have no interest in your past. I'm only interested in the here and now," Christian said.

"You need to care, Christian. My sullied past is unsuited to meld with your unblemished life. A secret like mine is corrosive. It will come between us, your family, Bianca. I must tell you everything about me, and you must decide if you still feel the same about me afterward. I will understand if you do not."

Part I

The Beginning

People, like a wisp of smoke, change with the shifting winds of time.

—M.L. Lexi

Chapter 1

WITH A FACE that knew more than most thirty-six-year-olds should, Toni told Christian her story. Hunched in his seat, Christian focused on listening to every word of Toni's surreal account of her life.

"And that is who I am, Christian. Now, do you understand why I ran away?" Toni stared at Christian.

Eyes fixed wide, Christian looked intently beyond him. Under the spill of a bright summer sun, the piazza teemed with tourists, cameras around their necks, and cell phones clicked to memorialize Milan's beauty. People sat around the edge of the circular fountain spewing water, soaking the sun, enjoying a gelato, or relaxing before resuming sightseeing. Boutiques of famous designers and cafés fringing the piazza burst at the seams with patrons.

Toni looked away to avoid the eyes that stared at her. "I am sorry to disappoint you this way, Christian, but I must tell you everything about me before you decide you want to be with me." Toni waved the black and white liveried waiter on when he came to the table and levelled her blue eyes at Christian. "My lifestyle, the one I have led until recently, for lack of knowing any different, is not something I want to introduce into your life. Unlike me, you have the perfect wholesome life and a loving family. I could not taint.... I know you say you are only interested in the here and now, but our past life creeps up when you least expect it and...."

Christian held a hand, palm out, to silence Toni.

In ordinary blue jeans and a white shirt, sleeves rolled to his elbows, no one would guess Christian to be the son of renowned fashion magnate Isabella Farfalla and Antonio Sabatini, the man known as the Canadian coffee king. Christian was tall like his father, Antonio. Much like Antonio, Christian was fit with an athletic body. His jet-black curls cascaded around a chiselled face with a dark stubble contrasting the sea-blue eyes.

"Give me a moment, please," Christian said, needing time to break down the information Toni dropped on his lap.

Closed-mouth, his mind rolling, Christian thought, contemplated, debated.

Christian looked at Toni. Her exceedingly blonde hair floated in shining waves around her beautiful face with large blue eyes, a full mouth painted fire-red, and skin with the outdoor colour look. The tauntingly sweet scent of her perfume reached deep into Christian and lingered there.

How does a man get past knowing the woman he loved, the woman he believed to be perfect, was pimped by her mother to support her extravagant lifestyle? How was Christian to move on from the revelation the woman he wanted to share his bed with had made it a practice of bedding rich men to extort them for money? Christ! How was he to get past the knowledge that the woman he wanted to marry had slept with as many men as she said she had?

It wasn't as if Christian was setting a double standard for Toni because she was a woman. Christian had no right to do so. Christian had as many women in his life as Toni had men. The difference was he hadn't targeted them for the sole purpose of blackmailing them. Compared to Toni, Christian spoiled the women in his life, and although his ultimate goal was sex, he was honest with them and treated them respectfully.

Situational ethics, he supposed that was.

Christian's dumbfounded face gave him away, and Toni made a noncommittal sound at the realization that their time had passed. Feeling immensely sad at the thought, Toni pushed back from the table and stood.

"I love you, Toni." Christian faltered. There was a moment of silence. Every woman's eyes in the café were on Christian. He could choose any of them, but his heart was Toni's, wholly and unconditionally. "I love you," Christian repeated.

"No, Christian, you do not. You cannot. You are a lovely man who does not deserve someone with a past like mine. I wish you nothing but love and happiness to fill your life. You deserve it." A solitary tear sprang from her eye and started down her face when she leaned down to touch her lips with his.

Christian reached for her hand to hold her back. "I do love you, and you're the only person who will fill my life with love and happiness."

Through a dim haze of confusion, Toni stared at him. "What are you saying, Christian?"

Christian indicated to Toni to sit in the chair she vacated. Toni sat.

"Everything you've told me is difficult to … process. It isn't easy to understand or accept a mother would do that to their child. How could she do that to you?" Christian raked edgy fingers through his hair.

Toni saw the bitterness and the anger that too often filled her take Christian over as it did her. It was a terrible burden for her to carry all these years, and now she imposed those feelings on the man she loved. Toni contaminated Christian's idyllic life, the only man who filled her life with love and treated her with kindness, with the imperfections that filled hers.

Christian's hand closed over Toni's when she started to tap her fingers on the tabletop as if playing the piano—a calming tactic she adopted long ago.

"I haven't been a saint either. Bianca is always keen to point out that I have pollinated half of the world's female population," Christian said.

On impulse, Toni lifted a single honey-brown eyebrow. "That is certainly ... something, but you cannot compare the two, Christian."

"Meaning to say, I haven't idly sat around saving myself for the special woman."

Shaking her head, Toni sighed heavily. "Christian, it is not the same thing. I...."

Christian cut in. "I only have one question. When you've been with me, did you do and say what you have for your mother, or did it come from you?"

"It came from me," she said swiftly, almost inaudibly. "I feel shame. I have always felt nothing but shame for my actions, but not with you, Christian."

Christian slid his fingers under her chin, turning her face to meet his. "I believe you, and you shouldn't feel ashamed or blame yourself. You trusted someone you love, someone who was your support system, and they used you and steered you in the wrong direction." Christian swiped the tears of hurt, regret, and betrayal that flowed heavily down Toni's cheeks with his thumb. "Know that I would never do you wrong. I'd never hurt you or make you cry. I'd go to the ends of this earth for you."

"Me too, Christian, but my past life is not something you introduce to people like you or your family."

"I want to be with you, and I think you want to be with me."

"I do, but...."

Christian abruptly bit off the rest of Toni's sentence. "I want you in my life. I want you in my bed at night. I want to wake up next to you every morning of my life. I want you to marry me, Toni." The tears came in sobs now, and Toni gasped for breath. "I asked her to marry me," Christian explained when those sitting at nearby tables turned with concerned eyes to look at Toni.

A slow smile spread across the French woman's face at the adjacent table. "Then you must do it properly. You must get down on one knee and ask her. *Allez. Allez.*" She made a rolling hand gesture to speed him along.

The café patio fell silent, and all eyes turned to Christian when he knelt and looked into Toni's eyes. "Toni Trevi, will you allow me to share your life and dreams? Will you make me a part of your days and nights? Will you make me the happiest man alive and marry me?" Christian removed his pinky ring and held it out to Toni.

The French woman's friend made a rolling motion with her forefinger to encourage Toni.

Toni shot up from her chair and into Christian's arms. "Yes. Yes, I will marry you."

AMID THE EXCITEMENT OF THE CLAPPING and cheering crowd, Toni failed to see her mother's eyes narrowed to thin slits, watching the blissful event unfold from the sideline. She watched one of the wealthiest and most eligible bachelors slide the ring on her daughter's finger. Michaela thought it was probably worth more than her tiny apartment.

Toni would be living her fairy tale dream all because of her. She'd introduced her daughter to Christian. She had concocted the scheme that led to Toni becoming his bed warmer. Toni's talents, honed from her schooling, took it from there.

She taught her daughter everything she knew, and Toni was betraying her. The resentment of betrayal from the daughter she'd cared for on her own since birth bubbled into seething anger in Michaela. It pushed Michaela to the edge, and everything throbbed at once.

After everything Michaela did for her daughter and the sacrifices she'd made, this was how Toni repaid her.

First, Toni turns her back on Michaela and goes home to live with that sorry excuse of a man she now calls Papa and his family. Michaela blamed Isabella for her daughter's duplicity. After all, Isabella put her worthless ex-husband, Joe Smith, who never saw anything through to the end, in touch with Toni. Michaela was sure Joe and his family had filled Toni's head with lies that drove her to refuse to take her calls.

Michaela damned Isabella and Joe.

Toni was her daughter, and Michaela wouldn't make her forget it anytime soon.

Chapter 2

AT BIANCA'S INSISTENCE, Christian's proposal to Toni followed a one-week stay at the Mesi Villa with Uncle Carlo and his wife Kat. Toni's father, Joe Smith, opened his home to the newly engaged couple. Joe told Christian they could stay as long as they wanted, but after finding out from Bianca who Joe was and knowing what he'd done to his mother, Christian declined the invitation. Joe was Toni's family, and Christian would have to forgive and forget in time, but it wasn't an option he was willing to visit yet.

Christian debated and considered what Antonio would say if he accepted Joe's dinner invitation that followed. Ultimately, Christian relented with much reluctance and only for Toni's sake.

Toni's newfound family attended the dinner at Joe's home, and the evening went better than Christian anticipated.

Francesca, Joe's wife and Toni's stepmother, was the whole package. She was a charming host, a great cook, and an Italian beauty who became the center of any room she walked into. Francesca had long, raven-black hair with straight-cut bangs over eyes that had soft laugh lines. Over the slim, medium-height frame, Francesca wore a flowing lilac skirt and a white silk blouse that was the essence of class and style.

Joe's sons, Massimo and Matteo, were the mirror image of their father in his younger years. Dark wavy hair fell around a tanned face with intelligent eyes and dimpled cheeks. Both men wore a black leather jacket over a white silk shirt and pleated black pants. Both men looked stylish and striking, as was the Italian way.

Matteo's wife Mia, whom Christian had met at the Milano Café and played a part in bringing Toni and him together, sat on the long, leather sofa. Mia was petite with a straight-cut bob that grazed her jawline and was a bouncy dark contrast to her fair face. Mia had almond-shaped eyes that saw through you. Matteo and Mia's two school-age, high-spirited boys were the spitting image of their stunning mother.

Nine years younger than Christian, Massimo enjoyed the company of women too much to fall into marriage. Massimo believed that variety was the spice of life. If Toni weren't his sister, Massimo would lecture Christian on the evils of committing himself to one woman.

Aurora was the baby of the family and the woman who worked in concert with Mia and Bianca to orchestrate the meeting between Toni and Christian at the Milano Café. Aurora inherited Francesca's good looks. Married to Riccardo, Aurora had a three-year-old daughter named Emilia. Both Aurora and Riccardo were in-demand architects who worked for the family business.

Joe's children, all accomplished professionals who worked in his successful construction business, led Christian to conclude Joe couldn't be all bad.

As was typical of any Italian dinner, it lasted hours. With a delectable six-course home-cooked meal prepared by Francesca, how could it not? There was great conversation, lots of wine, and laughter. Reminded of his mother's weekly family meals, Christian easily slid into the moment. But the bright look on Toni's face at her sense of belonging to a family that loved her made Christian overlook what Joe did years ago to his mother.

For Toni, Christian set aside his anger toward Joe for stalking his mother, the fear he'd instilled in her for years, and his assaults on her that led Isabella to question Bianca's origin.

The trials of love and loyalty, thought Christian, joining Joe in his study when invited for the one-on-one father-in-law and future son-in-law talk.

"Please have a seat, Christian." Joe waved him to the brown leather chair in the seating area of his study. "Will you join me in an after-dinner aperitif?"

Christian nodded and watched Joe pick up the monk-shaped bottle and pour the amber liquid into two shot glasses.

At sixty-seven, Joe's hair was elegantly gray at the temples, and his handsome face was lined with crevices etched by time. He wore an impeccably cut navy-blue Mesi suit over a tan shirt, and the perfectly knotted brown tie was silk. He exuded confidence and a distinguished air of polish.

Christian would feel underdressed if he weren't comfortable wearing jeans and a white shirt.

Christian watched Joe screw the lid onto the bottle and set it back into the mirrored bar section of the wall-to-ceiling bookcase overflowing with an eclectic selection of books and artifacts.

"That's quite the selection of reading material," Christian said to fill the deafening silence in the room dedicated as a home office.

"My work takes up most of my time. Francesca and the kids, mainly Aurora and Matteo, are the readers. Massimo's head has always been too crowded with women." Joe handed Christian his glass before he took a seat on the sofa.

A carved desk, polished to a shine, was clear except for a laptop, telephone, and blotter. Behind the desk sat a high-back leather chair. Two large windows on opposite sides of the desk displayed stunning handcrafted stained glass panels—a remnant from the building's once pious existence. The floors were dark slate tiles glossed to life when Joe bought the building.

"Understandable. Italy has many beautiful women to cause a man brain overload." Christian sipped some of the nutty-flavoured Frangelico.

"You speak from experience."

Christian sipped more Frangelico.

Joe flashed Christian a lopsided smirk. "Relax, Christian. I'm in no position to judge. We all have a past, and I'm no exception. Luckily, everything had a shelf life. Anyway, whatever time I can spare, I like to spend with my family, Francesca, and now with Toni. I must make up for the time I wasn't there for her." There was a softness to Joe's voice, regret in his eyes.

Damn, if the man wasn't chipping away at the anger that engendered the hate Christian had for Joe.

"Toni tells me you own a successful construction company." Christian took another swallow of his drink.

Joe nodded, tilting the lamp on the end table and fumbling out a cigarette and a pack of matches from its hollow bottom. "Three lecturing women in the house, now four with Toni." He explained touching a match to a cigarette and sucking it to life.

Christian would point out that the detectable cigarette smell was unavoidable, but he suspected Joe knew as much.

Joe exhaled a cloud of smoke. "After I managed to get my life together, I launched the company with…."

"My grandfather's money," Christian finished with a clipped tone. "I know the story, Signore Smith."

"Joe, please." Joe unearthed a tin ashtray from beneath the sofa and flicked ashes into it. "After all, we're soon to become family. And yes, you're right about it being your grandfather's money, but as you know, I repaid it when the opportunity presented itself. Anyway, it's why I wanted to speak to you." Joe sent the drink streaming down his throat. Liquid courage. "It's clear to me you love Toni."

Christian looked straight into Joe's eyes. "I do, sir. The fact that I'm here proves it."

Joe studied him through the haze of exhaled smoke. "Yes, I suppose coming tonight was difficult for you, and as much as that deserves a conversation, we'll have to leave it for another day." Joe rose, picked up the cognac bottle and two glasses, and brought them to the sitting area. The conversation required a strong drink. "Tonight, I want to talk to you about protecting my daughter from her mother, my ex-wife Michaela."

The conversation took a turn Christian didn't expect, and it showed on his face. "What do you mean?"

Joe waved the bottle at Christian before pouring VSOP into the two glasses. "Just that. I want you to give me your word you will protect Toni."

"Of course I will. You have my word. I would never let anything happen to Toni, but what do you expect to happen?" Christian rested a perplexed look on Joe.

"I don't know exactly." Contemplatively, Joe stared down at the liquid in his glass. "What I do know is that my daughter is marrying a very wealthy man, and that's a magnet for Michaela to do anything and everything to get her hands on your money. What I do know is that you are Isabella's son, whom she envies and resents with every fibre of her being. What I do know is that Michaela detests me as much as she does your mother."

Christian watched Joe crush the cigarette on the ashtray and take a sizeable, numbing gulp of his drink.

"Now that I'm in Toni's life, it's safe to presume Michaela's rage has swelled tenfold. Protecting her from Michaela's reach is what I need to do. I didn't protect my daughter for years because I didn't know of her existence, and Michaela forced her to…." Unable to say the words,

Joe fell silent, fisting his hand in anger as the pain came to him.

Christian fell into the silence with Joe.

Christian imagined a father's ache and overwhelming guilt at knowing the dreadful things his daughter was brainwashed into doing. Christian identified with Joe's deadened grief and helplessness at not being there for Toni.

"Toni's told me everything. She said you told her that a secret is a corrosive thing to come between two people and opened up to me," Christian said after the heavy silence lingered.

A faint smile flickered in Joe's eyes. "Brave girl and smart."

"She's all that."

"If Toni's told you everything, then you know what her mother is capable of."

"I do, and I can assure you I won't allow anything to happen to Toni."

Joe looked deep into Christian's eyes and knew he meant it. Seeing an ally in Christian, the heavy burden of distress weighing Joe down lifted off his shoulders.

Joe rubbed his eyes with his thumb and forefinger. "Thank you, Christian. That means a lot. I couldn't protect my daughter then. Now that she's in my life, I will not risk her loss and will protect her no matter what it takes."

"Me too, sir." Christian held his glass up, and crystal rang against crystal.

Before it swung open, there was a knock on the door, and both men turned to see Toni. "Sorry to interrupt, but Francesca wants the two of you in the living room for coffee and cake." Toni turned to Christian. "She baked us an engagement cake, a two-tier vanilla-pistachio cake. She spent all afternoon making it." Toni smiled warmly.

That someone had spent time and effort to do something nice for her was a new and wonderful concept.

"Sure, honey. We're done here." Joe rose, pecked Toni on the cheek, and left the room.

"What did he say to you?" asked Toni.

"To take care of you, or I'd have to answer to him. And I promised him I would." Christian brushed his lips to Toni's.

Toni's smile brightened. "It is nice to know so many people are looking out for me. Come on. We have a cake to eat, although I do not know how I can eat any more food."

Chapter 3

THE DRIVER WOUND the car past the entrance, down the long cobbled road that led to a curving driveway and stopped in front of Isabella's house, a Victorian red brick façade that rose two stories. The entryway was arched, tall, and stately. Expansive windows were framed in black, and a blooming garden dropping with colour bordered the house. To the left of the house, the four-car garage housed Antonio's prized Ferrari, Lamborghini, and two less sporty cars.

Christian alighted the car and turned his face up to the hot sun. He breathed in the scents of summer, floating under a warm breeze. Christian could smell freshly mowed grass, lilac, and roses that painted the air. Trees lining the driveway and those on the expanse of land enveloping the house were crowned in the fresh green of the season. As far as the eye could see, the grass was a smooth, verdant carpet.

Milan was great, but home was better, Christian thought with a smile.

"You go on in, Christian. I'll get the suitcases," said Jose, Isabella's long-time driver, opening the car's trunk. "Go on. Your mother has been waiting for you. They all have."

Christian nodded. "Thanks, Jose."

Reaching for Toni's hand, Christian started for the front door, and she stopped him. "I do not know if I can do this, Christian. I do not know if I am ready."

Across the span of weeks, Toni's life had changed unimaginably. She met the father she wasn't sure existed.

She found out she had brothers and sisters, nieces and nephews. Toni found a family that accepted, welcomed, and loved her. Toni became engaged to a man who wanted nothing from her but to love, protect, and fill her with happiness. As good as those changes were, they revealed how misguided Toni's life had been.

Until recently, Toni's life had been in a downward spiral of depravity. Until now, Toni hadn't realized her entire life had been but a lie and an extraordinary exaggeration. Toni felt ashamed of her life and of who she was.

At this time in her life—the happiest she had ever been—her mother was still sabotaging her happiness.

"You are ready for this," Christian assured Toni.

"I do not know." Toni wondered if she could ever put her past behind her.

"You are, and I'm right here with you. Trust me." Christian glided his lips over Toni's and smoothed her fears.

"I trust you," Toni said.

Christian led Toni through the front door, past the foyer, and to the large chef's kitchen, where he knew he would find his grandmother and mother and their maid, Marisol.

Christian smelled spicy tomato sauce, sautéed garlic, and baked bread. His mouth watered.

Bowls, a cutting board, the makings for bruschetta, a salad, and garlic bread covered the countertop. Next to the pasta maker, propped against the edge of the table, were mountains of rolled fettuccine. Four pots steamed simultaneously on the gas stove, and the double ovens were fit to burst with a glazed ham, eggplant and cutlet parmigiana, and cannelloni.

Amidst the banging and the whirr of the mixer, no one saw Christian and Toni standing at the doorway. "How long until we eat? I'm starving," Christian said.

Isabella turned first. Her chestnut hair was caught into a ponytail, and her cheeks were flushed red with heat. She wore a simple, understated white flowing dress with a thick black belt and looked stunning. Isabella looked every bit the fashionista she was.

Isabella's mouth spread wide with a smile. "You're here."

Christian walked up to his mother and took her into a fierce hug after pecking her on the cheek. "Came straight here from the airport with…." Christian put his hand out and Toni walked up slowly and met it, "My fiancée."

Shame edging on Toni's face, she caught her cherry-red painted bottom lip between her teeth. "Hello, Mrs. Farfalla."

Toni looked down to the ground when she felt the weight of Isabella's expressionless dark eyes burn into her.

Isabella's eyes roamed Toni's face. Toni's blonde hair, now shaded chestnut, hung loosely around a face bronzed by the sun. Her tanned bare legs flashed under the short, white pleated skirt topped with a mustard-yellow blouse with black circles. At her feet, she wore flats.

"You've changed your hair," Isabella said.

"*Si.* Yes. I wanted a new look for my new life." Toni had the look of bottled tension that you have when meeting the in-laws for the first time, although hers was there for a different reason.

"I think she looks great," Christian said, pecking Maria and Marisol, who now turned their attention away from the ham in the oven and grating cheese to him. "Doesn't my fiancée look beautiful, Gran?"

"She certainly does?" Maria excitedly ran her hands over her peppered hair to tuck the flyaway strands and smoothed the front of her floral dress before taking Toni into a tight embrace. "You two are going to have beautiful babies."

A smile played across Marisol's round face. "*Si, Señora* Maria, they will have beautiful, beautiful babies, and I will look after them. It's been a long time since we have babies in this house."

"It has been a long time and you will only look after them when I'm not, Marisol." Isabella stepped between Maria and Marisol and brushed back the hair that curtained Toni's face. "I like the change."

Toni's tightened face loosened. "You do. That means a lot coming from you, Mrs. Farfalla."

Isabella smiled at Toni. "Mmm-hmm, I am all about new beginnings. And you can call me Isabella or Mom, but not Mrs. Farfalla. It makes me sound old. Welcome to the family, honey." Isabella wrapped her arms around Toni, and Toni felt her tension and irrational fear vaporize.

"You call me Gran." Maria linked arms with Christian and Toni. "Now you, too, go freshen up. Everyone should be here soon to celebrate the greatest achievement on earth." Maria turned to whisper in Toni's ear and watched Toni's lips bloom into that blushing smile that always made Christian's heart skip a beat.

"What did Gran say to you back there?" Christian asked.

Half turning, Toni said, "That tonight we celebrate the woman who managed to get her grandson to settle down, and if we like, we could start working on making her those great grandbabies now."

Christian laughed. "I told you the women in my family don't hold back." He took Toni's hand and aimed his eyes up the winding staircase. "I do still have a bedroom here."

Chapter 4

THEY ALL CAME, including Romeo, the floppy ear Maltese with round dark eyes. All convened at Isabella's dining table, the center of every family gathering over three decades. Light spilled bright from the grand crystal ceiling chandelier over the room. The damask curtains at the picture windows were pulled open, revealing an orange sky as dusk settled in and shadows began to stretch across the land.

The dining room was expansive and commensurate with the stately home, but it felt homey to Toni. The long table adorned with a vintage ivory tablecloth, fine dinnerware, and Baccarat glassware overflowed with the food Isabella, Maria, and Marisol had prepared all day. There were bowls of salads and silver platters with ham, cutlet and eggplant parmigiana. The pasta eaters had the option of ricotta stuffed cannelloni in cream sauce and spaghetti in tomato sauce. There were red and white bottles of wine for the adults and milk for the girls. Four white candles speared from silver candleholders.

Scanning the table, Toni looked at the upstanding, over-accomplished group who came to celebrate her engagement to Christian without judgment. Approval, a once implausible notion, was no longer a far-fetched dream for Toni. Toni's stars aligned after thirty-six very long, very miserable years of her life. Toni was finally blessed with good-hearted, loving people who put her on a new path and demanded nothing of her in return.

The group gathered here tonight was family.

Bianca, Isabella's daughter and now the head of the Farfalla Empire, sat next to her husband, Lorenzo. Isabella chose steadfast, loyal Lorenzo to replace her as the head designer when she stepped into retirement. Bianca and Lorenzo sat beside their girls, Rosanna, ten and Serena, seven.

There was Gail and her husband, Marco. Gail, Isabella's long-time friend-slash-assistant, stood by Isabella since she launched *Isabella Farfalla Fashion* without a penny to her name. Gail weathered Isabella's struggles and financial challenges and stood by her through the bad times. No matter how difficult Gail was there. In recognition of her loyalty, Isabella signed over ten percent of her company to Gail, making her a wealthy woman. Gail's husband, Marco, worked as a waiter for Antonio at his first *The Café* restaurant. Now, he was the franchise owner of a dozen of the fifteen hundred *The Café* restaurants worldwide.

At the head of the table, Salvatore Mesi, Isabella's father, sat next to his wife, Maria. Their love story was as remarkable as the Mesi name, which Sal built into a worldwide fashion brand. Sal's son Carlo took over the company years ago and continued his legacy with equal success.

Tall and handsome, a self-made man, Antonio Sabatini sat at the opposite end of the table. Antonio's dark hair, with distinguishing flecks of gray at the temples, was neatly combed back. Character lines fanned from the intelligent blue eyes, and beneath the burgundy shirt and black dress pants, his body was trim and fit at sixty-eight.

Antonio was still working through the shock of Christian's unexpected engagement and the fact he'd soon become family with Joe Smith, the man who stalked and assaulted Isabella decades ago.

Why the surreal turn of events took Antonio aback was a surprise in itself. Whenever Isabella and their daughter Bianca plotted together, the consequence was too often a melodramatic Shakespearean ending. The strong, independent, and overly confident women in his family had a mind of their own were going to be the death of him. As burdensome as that was, Antonio wouldn't have it any other way.

Standing, Antonio clinked his spoon on crystal, getting everyone's attention, including excited barks from Romeo. The ham bone Antonio tossed Romeo quieted him and sent him scurrying under the table to feast on it.

"Goddamn dog knows how to play me every time," Antonio murmured, eliciting a smile from Isabella.

Antonio continued.

"Everyone, please raise your glass to my son and Toni, the woman who managed to bring him to his senses." Antonio looked pointedly at his son with a raised brow and turned to Toni. "That you managed such an impossible feat tells me you are the type of strong, intelligent woman he needs in his life." Antonio turned his gaze back to Christian. "Every man needs the love and support of his family, and you will always have that, unconditionally. But a loving, supportive partner sharing your life and dreams and standing by you," Antonio reached for Isabella's hand, "Makes all your successes more meaningful, and this ride called life a worthwhile experience."

Sal's hand moved to rest on Maria's. "Here. Here."

Antonio turned blue eyes to Toni. "Isabella and I, the family at this table tonight, categorically welcome you with open arms and hearts."

"To Toni and Christian," said everyone simultaneously, raising their glasses.

Serena slid off her chair and made a B-line to Christian. "Uncle Chris, am I going to be your bridesmaid?"

"Baby, I think that's Toni's decision," Christian said.

Serena turned to Toni. "Toni?" She bit down on her lip and slipped into a moment of contemplative silence. "Do I call you Toni or Auntie Toni?"

Toni's heart melted, and she faltered. Her expression underwent that transformation that proceeded to tears, but she blinked them back. "You can call me what makes your heart happy," Toni said.

"Auntie Toni makes me happy. Am I going to be your bridesmaid?" Serena said.

Toni brushed dark hair from Serena's face and tucked it behind her ear. "I was thinking of a better role for you, *amore*. What do you think of being a flower girl? You will wear a pretty dress and carry flower petals in a basket to scatter down the aisle." Toni watched Serena's face bloom into an expression of delight.

"I can do that. I will scatter petals everywhere. Can my dress have a bow? I like bows." Serena's voice rose in her escalating excitement.

"Sure it can. How about a big frilly bow around your waist that ties at your back?" Toni said, making the child's eyes widen in wonder.

"I'll help you design it," Isabella offered. "And I'd like to design your wedding gown too, Toni. If you like?"

Now, Toni's eyes popped wide. "I would like that very much. Thank you, Isabella."

"Woah! I'm going to wear an original Farfalla flower girl dress." Serena's comment had the room in smiles.

"You and me both." Toni's voice was as excited as Serena's.

"You can talk about this later. We have an engagement cake to eat, and I don't want anyone claiming diet." Marisol rolled into the dining room, pushing a cart with the three-tier chocolate cake with white icing and colourful-piped flowers she and Maria had worked on the past three days.

Big, silent tears coursed down Toni's face. It was the second cake in one week someone had made for her for no reason other than to make her heart swell.

"You don't need to cry, Auntie Toni. Nana and Marisol make the best yummy cakes," Serena said.

Christian lifted Serena and sat her on his lap. "She knows it will be delicious, baby. It's not why she's crying."

"Why is she crying?" Antonio whispered in Isabella's ears.

"Because it makes her feel loved and safe. Because her life is filled with a family, she didn't believe it was possible. Because she's filled with a wonderful peace, she didn't know until now." Isabella enlightened her husband. *And I pray it stays that way.*

Chapter 5

IT WAS RAINING low and steady under a dark sky. Toni's silver Porsche, Christian's engagement gift, was parked in front of Bianca's home, raindrops bouncing off it.

Toni walked to Bianca's front door, and for the second time, Toni dawdled and returned to the car.

After several steps, Toni stopped. Oblivious to the rain that fell and drenched her to the bone, Toni had a long conversation with herself. After the one-sided conversation, Toni climbed the slate steps leading to Bianca's front door for the third time. Toni's steps were slow, and she paused when she reached the top step.

Toni returned to the car.

"*Amore*, should you not put her out of her misery?" Lorenzo stood next to Bianca at the living room window, watching Toni walk toward the front door and away several times.

"Do you think I should? Maybe she must decide on her own whether to knock on the door." Bianca stepped away from the window when the heavy rain obstructed the view.

"Do you know why she has come?"

"I have no idea, but you're right. I should put her out of her misery." Bianca handed Lorenzo her cognac glass. "I'll get the door. She's getting soaked. Imagine what Christian will do to me if Toni catches the sniffles."

"Oh, hello." Toni looked at Bianca as if startled by a reverie when the front door swung open.

The pink short-sleeve floral print dress Toni wore hung heavy with rain. Toni's chestnut hair was plastered wet on her head.

"Come in from under the rain." Bianca's smile was wide and welcoming as she pushed open the door and stepped aside.

Bianca's hair was bound into a smooth ponytail. In skinny jeans, a mustard-yellow tank top, and flat patent ballerina shoes, Bianca looked as graceful and elegant as in her office attire and as formidable and intimidating.

"I hope I am not bothering you."

"You're not. You're always welcome here, Toni." Bianca closed the door behind them.

Toni looked down at the pool of water spreading at her feet. "I am sorry."

"No problem. That's small compared to the puddle the girls and Romeo left behind half an hour ago." A smile played across Bianca's face. "Let's get you into dry clothes."

Toni mirrored Bianca's smile. "Thank you. That would be nice."

Toni's wet hair was wrapped in a towel as she entered the study. Toni had changed into plum leggings, a hoodie, and white running shoes.

"I thought you could use this." Bianca handed Toni a warm cognac.

"Yes. Thank you." Toni sat on the sofa in the sitting area, and Bianca settled into the matching chair beside her.

"So, tell me, what can I do for you?" Bianca crossed one slender leg over another.

Silently, Bianca watched Toni play with the marquise-cut ruby engagement ring Christian asked her to help select and slid on her finger only days ago.

Toni drank half the cognac in a single pull. "I was wondering, Bianca, if I could...." Toni stopped. She drank some more.

"Toni, say what's on your mind," Bianca said when Toni fell silent. "We're family now, which entitles you to say what you think. It's how our family works. My mother has always encouraged open and honest communication."

Toni tossed back the rest of the cognac in her glass. "I know it is a lot for me to ask, and I will understand if you say no."

"Go on, Toni. Ask away." Bianca encouraged.

"I wondered if you would consider ah.... You can say no, Bianca. I just wanted...."

Bianca made a rolling motion with her forefinger to encourage Toni when she hesitated.

"I would like to work for you again, you know, as your assistant." Toni read the look Bianca shot her as repudiation, not for the surprised look it was. "I understand you do not trust me."

"It's not that, Toni. You can afford not to work. I thought you wouldn't want to."

Pleased she misread Bianca, Toni broke in with a happy laugh. "Oh, no, I would like to work. I am not—how do you say?—the woman of the house type."

"I think you mean the housewife type," Bianca said after some thought. "Understandable. I'm not either."

"And I would like to work with you, Bianca. And if it is possible. I would also like to take over the Ming Project again. Only if possible, of course. I do not want to step on anyone's toes."

"Margie, Carole, and Suzanne are managing the program now."

The rain had stopped, and the dew skimmed over the ground and grass and hung from leaves. The smell of rich, wet earth hung in the air. Dark clouds were moving out, and the sun was starting to peek out to spill sunshine over the land.

Toni rose to expend nervous energy and walked to the window. "Then I will work with them. As I said, I do not want to overstep, especially now that I am marrying Christian. I do not want to get preferential treatment." Toni picked up the cognac bottle and refilled their glasses.

"As family, I can find you a more important role in the company that comes with a title."

Toni corked the bottle and set it down on the coffee table before she sat back down. "I am not interested in appearances, Bianca, and I do not say it out of a sense of being good. I liked being your assistant. As you say, I do it well. I would rather do something well than badly for a title."

Bianca met Toni's eyes. A moment of respect crossed between them. "All right. I'd be happy to have you back as my assistant, and you can work with Margie, Carole, and Suzanne on the Ming Project. I'm sure they'll relinquish it to you in time. They have a lot on their plate as is. You must remember, Toni, that we're employer and employee at the office, not sisters-in-law."

Toni grinned happily. "Yes. Yes, of course, I understand. Thank you, Bianca. I assure you, you can trust me not to betray you ever again," Toni embarrassedly assured.

"I know you won't. I have every faith in you, Toni," Bianca said in a persuasive voice to placate the unconvinced look on Toni's face.

Toni understood trust wasn't redeemable through mere words. Toni had to prove herself to Bianca and would.

There was a knock, and Rosanna and Serena poked their heads around the door.

"I told you she was here, Rosy," Serena announced excitedly and lunged on the sofa beside Toni. "Hi, Auntie Toni, are you here to go swimming with us?"

"Mom wants us to practice piano, but I'd rather go swimming." Rosanna fell back on the sofa and crossed her arms on her chest.

Serena leaned in to whisper in Toni's ear. "Mommy doesn't know it, but I have my bathing suit under my shorts and T-shirt. Don't tell her."

"I am sorry, *amore*, I did not bring my bathing suit."

"Mommy has lots of bathing suits. Her boobies aren't as big as yours, but it's okay because it'll be just us girls swimming. And Romeo," Serena said when he raced forward with his tongue lolling and lunged onto the sofa. "He's a boy, but he's a dog and doesn't care about boobies."

Romeo barked in agreement.

"That is good to know." Toni scratched Romeo's head.

Bianca's eyebrows lifted. "Well, thank you for that observation, Serena."

Rosanna guffawed. "It's true, Mom. You're always complaining about how small your boobs are. I hope mine blow up bigger than that." Rosanna eyed her mother's chest.

"All right, that's enough boob talk from you two." Bianca's eyes caught Toni's. "If you'd like to take the girls swimming, we can find you a bathing suit that fits."

Stifling a smile, Toni said, "I would like that. We'll have to wait until it stops raining."

"Fine," Serena said with a jab of disappointment.

"How about we make it a family night? I'll have everyone join us for dinner." Bianca offered. "Afterward, Toni, you and I can sit down, and I'll read you in on what you're returning to at work."

Serena jumped in before Toni could answer Bianca. "Can we have hot dogs and hamburgers with potato chips, Mommy?"

"How about a compromise, hamburgers and hot dogs with potato salad." Bianca offered and watched her daughters conferring with one another through eye contact.

Rosanna sighed and firmed her lips. "Fine. Potato salad instead of chips,"

Bianca twisted up her lips. "Good doing business with you. I'll have Nanny make your favourite potato salad and…."

Life didn't seem to hold much promise for a long while, but today, the girls, family, and talk of the job that meant everything to Toni was Toni's life now, and it couldn't be more perfect.

Chapter 6

ARMS FOLDED, CHRISTIAN leaned against the door and watched Toni reach into the closet for the umpteenth outfit. Holding the cream blouse and brown pants against her, she eyed herself in the floor-length mirror and turned to Christian. Christian saw only the white lace thong and matching bra painted over the female curves.

"It looks as good as the fifteen previous outfits." Christian brushed his lips to hers.

"You are just saying that." Toni tossed the blouse and pants on the pile of clothes, amassing into a tall mountain on the bed.

"This body looks great in anything." Christian gave Toni's butt a suggestive squeeze. "I can think of something better to do now than go through your closet."

Toni batted away Christian's hand. "This is important. It is my first day back to work since I betrayed my friends and your sister, and every eye in the place will be on me. The judgment will be worse now that I am engaged to you. I must look professional...." Toni rambled on without taking a breath before turning back to the closet.

"It's a job, Toni. Bianca doesn't care what you look like. All she wants is for you to do a great job. She's been through four assistants since you left, and she wants stability and someone to organize her work life and office." Christian rolled up the sleeves of his white silk shirt to his elbows and tucked it into his jeans. "As for everyone else, for as long as there are human beings, gossip will be a part of office life. My best advice is to ignore it. I do."

Toni poked her head out of the closet. "What have you heard?"

"Nothing about you, not that anyone would talk to me about you. I'm talking from experience. I'm the owner's son and a sex god. The staff talks about this," Christian ran his hands over his body, "Often."

Toni guffawed. "I am serious, Christian."

"I know, but you need to focus only on the job because that will bring you a sense of satisfaction. Gossip will not."

"Yes. You are right," Toni said, with a long sigh, and reached for the cream blouse and brown ankle-high pants at the top of the pile on the bed.

"Perfect choice," Christian said. "Anyway, I'm driving you to work. I don't trust you behind the wheel of a car today. I'll see you downstairs in half an hour."

"Okay," Toni said, turning back to the closet.

"Half an hour, Toni, or you'll be late on your first day back." Christian paused at the door before walking out of the bedroom.

"Yes. I heard you."

Toni accessorized with spiked backless heels, gold at her neck, and hoops at her ears. Toni twisted and turned in front of the mirror. With a nod of approval, Toni went downstairs.

Chapter 7

IT TOOK TONI no time to slide back into the role of Bianca's assistant, but it would take time and effort to gain the trust of her former colleagues. Being engaged to the founder's son didn't guarantee the alliances of colleagues she had let down.

Turning the information over to her mother that she used to blackmail Bianca strained Toni's relationship with Margie, Carole, and Suzanne, her only true friends. Toni had to regain their trust and vowed to do so. She only had to figure out how to do it.

Catching up to the workload was another matter. Bianca's productive and diligent work ethic generated more work than the combined CEOs Toni had worked for over the years.

Toni's desk was piled high with unread files, unfinished reports, unanswered emails, and scheduling conflicts left by her predecessor clearly over his head. Toni met the challenge with exuberant delight.

Toni settled into the chair behind the L-shaped mahogany desk and got to work. Toni got herself read-in on all the active files and documents. Toni caught up on Bianca's many projects on the go, completed the unfinished reports, answered unaddressed emails, and junked the nonsense. Toni sorted Bianca's calendar. She cancelled unnecessary meetings and rescheduled the necessary ones to more cohesive times.

After three weeks of working fourteen-hour days, Toni got caught up. Toni sat back and eyed the clean, neat desk with pride. Toni could see the polished mahogany desktop for the first time, and Bianca's office was running smoothly and on track again.

A smile touched Toni's mouth at the notion she proved she wasn't incapable of realizing an objective, as her mother so often pointed out.

For a moment, Toni wrapped her mind in thoughts of her mother. It had been months since Toni last spoke to Michaela. Since then, Toni's life trajectory changed for the better.

Toni found the father she had wondered about all of her life. She was united with brothers and sisters she didn't know she had. Toni now had a stepmother who welcomed her into the family with open arms. As if all that wasn't goodness enough, Toni was engaged to a wonderful, loving man who overlooked the woman she was and encouraged the woman she could be.

Life was great without her mother, and Toni aimed to keep it that way.

Caught up at work, Toni focused on planning her Christmas wedding. Toni intended to have a small affair with family and, hopefully, some work friends. Isabella, however, insisted on a lavish affair. Eventually, Toni had no choice but to relent to Isabella. Toni would have a church wedding, wear a beautiful Mikado silk gown, and have a lavish reception with family.

Antonio still had to come to terms with Joe Smith becoming a part of the family, but he didn't stand in Isabella's way when she offered the corporate jet to fly Joe Smith and his family to the wedding. Toni deserved happiness in her life, as did his son.

After the Sunday family dinner at Isabella's home, everyone retired to the living room while Toni sat with Isabella in the study. Lamps and the ceiling light lit the room bright. Outside, the sky was dark, and the light rain from it drifted a little on the soft wind. The smell of wet soil and grass painted in the night air.

"This is what I have so far." Isabella handed Toni the pencilled sketches.

Speechless for a long while, Toni stared at the sketch of the floor-sweeping slip-style dress with shoestring straps and a plunging back. She scanned over the design of the pink tulip dress with the white waist sash that tied into a flowing bow at the back.

"That one is meant for the flower girls," Isabella said.

"Flower girls." Toni stretched out the *S* for emphasis.

Isabella's skin looked darkly tanned in the white flowing dress with shoulder straps. "I know you told Serena she would be your flower girl, but I don't think she'd be upset if Emilia, Aurora's daughter, joined her."

A frown brought Toni's brows together. "You do not think she would?"

"No, honey, she wouldn't. Besides, it's your wedding, and you should do what you want," Isabella said. "You should have whomever you like at your wedding. You should have your family with you to celebrate your happy day."

"I did not want to upset Serena by suggesting it."

"I know, but she's a child, honey. She gets distracted by the mention of candy." Amusement touched Isabella's mouth, and Toni mirrored it. "This is the dress I envisioned for the bridesmaids and maid of honour."

"This looks like a child's dress," Toni said of the blush trumpet V-neck dress.

"It is. This is the adult version of the dress." Isabella held the sketch up for Toni to see. "It's long with a sweeping train, a slit that shows a lot of leg, and rushing at the waist, just in case you wanted to ask Aurora and Mia to be a bridesmaid along with Rosanna."

Toni turned her head toward Isabella and stared at her. "How did you know that is what I was planning to do?"

"I've been involved with thousands of brides over the years, and reading my bride is my specialty."

Toni held a sketch in each hand and flicked eyes from one to the other. "So, you know I would like to ask Bianca to be my maid of honour."

Isabella nodded. "I do. She's the oldest of the group."

"I think I must fear your mind-reading skills, Isabella?" Toni spread the sketches on the coffee table to eye over.

"Only when I'm not drinking, which isn't often." Isabella drank the rest of her martini, picked up the skewered olive, and set it between her teeth.

Both women burst out laughing.

"They are beautiful, Isabella. Stunning, and it is exactly what I want."

"I know you're not just saying that, but if you'd like anything changed, I want you to be honest."

"I do not want anything changed. Nothing at all." Toni leaned in and wrapped her arms around Isabella. "Thank you."

"All right then. I thought we'd make the dresses out of chiffon fabric. Of course, your dress will be made from Mikado silk…."

"Mommy says we're having dessert, and if you'd like some to get your butt into the living room," Serena announced, walking into the study.

"What have we said about knocking on doors before entering a room?" Isabella said.

"Oh, yeah. Come on, Romeo." Serena walked out of the room with Romeo, knocked on the door, and waited for Isabella's acknowledgement.

"Come in," Isabella called out, watching Serena walk into the room and Romeo race forward with his tongue lolling. "Yes, Serena, what is it?"

"Mommy is serving dessert and coffee in the living room if you and Auntie Toni would like some." Serena hopped on the sofa between Toni and Isabella, and Romeo followed suit.

"So, she didn't say, 'Get your butt into the living room?'" Isabella rubbed Romeo's ears and kissed his shaggy head.

They could see Serena thinking about the question and her answer. "I remembered now that Mommy said that to Rosanna and me." Serena caught sight of the sketches and noticed the pink dress with the bow at the waist. "Is this the dress I'm wearing to your wedding?"

"It is, *amore*. Do you like it?"

"It's pretty. I'm going to look great in it," Serena exclaimed enthusiastically.

Tucking a strand of Serena's dark hair behind her ear, Toni said, "Would you be upset if a second flower girl walked down the aisle with you?"

Serena looked into Toni's eyes. "Would I still be throwing flowers on the carpet and wearing this dress?"

"Petals, and yes, you will both be wearing the same dress."

"Okay, Auntie Toni. I want to throw stuff on the floor. Mommy doesn't let me do that here."

"Well, you and Emilia can throw all the rose petals you like."

Serena's eyes were bright. "Can Romeo be a flower dog? He knows how to throw stuff on the floor real good?"

"Well … umm." Unknowing how to respond, Toni looked at Isabella.

"Candy," was all Isabella said.

"Do you have any, Nana? You know those big round gumballs?"

"I do, baby. Fetch my handbag on the foyer table."

"Sure, Nana. Come on, Romeo. We're getting candy."

"Thank you," Toni mouthed at Isabella.

"Don't mention it, honey. A child's attention span is a wondrous thing," Isabella said, watching Serena skip out of the room with Romeo following.

"I meant for sketching the dresses, for … everything, Isabella. I know it was not easy for you to do what you did, especially after—you know?—what Papa did to you all those years ago," Toni murmured. "He told me everything, and I am so sorry."

"That's between your father and me. You weren't the cause, and that's in the past, honey. I forgave your father long ago." Antonio is another issue, but that's neither here nor there, Isabella thought. "Forgiveness sets you free to love, and there's no need for thanks." Isabella rested her hand on Toni's. "I only ask that you make my boy happy."

"I promise you, I will do my best to make Christian happy."

Chapter 8

ON HER HONEYMOON almost forty years ago, Michaela fell in love with everything that was Venice. After all these years, and as much as Michaela enjoyed living in Venice, she never got used to the constant noise from the influx of tourists. This morning was no exception as the incessant chatter from people sightseeing on the warm summer morning flowed into the apartment and distracted Michaela.

"Christ, what could these morons possibly have to say of interest or consequence that they can't say in their hotel room. Shut the fuck up?" Michaela screamed to the crowds below before slamming the doors to the balcony overlooking the canal shut.

At sixty-six, Michaela took great care of herself and looked fifteen years younger. It was seven o'clock in the morning, yet Michaela's face was expertly made up, and her wide, pouty mouth was painted the trademark cherry red. She wore a very tight, very short white dress. There were diamonds at her ears and neck, gold bracelets on her wrist, and a ruby ring on her left hand. All gifts she acquired from the many lovers gratified over the years. She had the type of big blue eyes that could charm any man she wanted into her lair.

Michaela's apartment, acquired with Sal Mesi's bribe money before Isabella cut her off with lies and trickery, was a luxurious oasis of comfort. The spiral staircase led up to two bedrooms. High beamed ceilings, Venetian terrazzo flooring, white walls, and blue lace curtains on the main floor lent to a nautical decor. The kitchen Michaela used only to brew coffee was a state-of-the-art envy of any chef. Appearance was everything to Michaela.

Michaela poured Chianti into a crystal glass and walked to the living room. Sitting on the buttery-soft leather couch, she sipped wine and fired up her laptop. When the screen brightened, Michaela checked her emails. Michaela immediately spotted Sheldon Tanner of ST Investigators's email and clicked it open.

Hey Baby Cakes,

Take a look at the video attachment. I'm sorry it took so long to get it to you. I was out of town on business and came across the video on my desk when I returned. Anyway, I think it will interest you.

I'm craving your naked body and talent. Let me know when you're in town.

Sheldon

Men were simple and easily manipulated, Michaela thought. Sleep with a man, praise their performance, and you can get them to do anything without doling out a cent.

Sheldon Tanner, sleuth extraordinaire, was no exception.

Michaela honed in on Sheldon Tanner fifteen ago when on a family vacation in Venice. The services of a top-notch private investigator always came in handy.

At best, an average lover—as most men were—Michaela made Sheldon believe otherwise. Michaela did things to him and for him that his wife never would. Sheldon's appreciation for Michaela's talent got her free investigation services from his top-notch firm. Once again, Sheldon came through when Michaela asked him to spy on her daughter's whereabouts.

Tipping the glass to her lips, Michaela drank deeply before pressing play on her laptop. Modern technology is marvellous; it could be intrusive with little detection, Michaela thought as the video came to life on the laptop's screen.

Michaela stared at the video of the family cozily gathered at Isabella's mansion, in her massive dining room, for dinner to celebrate Toni's engagement to Christian—without her. Michaela's eyes blazed red with anger when she caught Isabella, all smiles and pride for her family, and Toni sitting beside her.

"My, Daughter, you bitch. Mine." Michaela hissed between her teeth, slamming the laptop close.

When Michaela calmed down, she flipped the laptop open. Michaela's eyes focused on the video. She watched Bianca, her hair pulled back tightly to expose the face, which had barely a trace of makeup.

"Who walks around without makeup?" Michaela scoffed.

Bianca could afford decent face paint with the kind of money she had. It boggled Michaela to see Lorenzo adoringly stare at Bianca, looking as she did.

Michaela eyed Gail and her waiter husband. Professional hangers-on, Michaela concluded. Too stupid to see through their game, Isabella rewarded Gail with a share of her company. Isabella would instead give to a stranger than family.

"Goddamn it, I'm family, blood," Michaela barked at the screen.

Michaela's anger waned when Antonio came into the frame. Michaela's love-struck eyes fixed on him. Antonio still looked good enough to eat. Standing at the head of the table, Antonio looked authoritative and gorgeous. Michaela rested her chin on her bent knees and watched Antonio with tender eyes.

Michaela rewound and played over and over, watching Antonio, only him.

Antonio's low-pitched, dulcet voice sent shivers up Michaela's spine and made her insides simmer. Instant heat, instant need burst through Michaela. Lust speared into her hot and sharp. Michaela felt herself go wet.

Michaela heard Antonio say: A loving, supportive partner sharing your life and dreams and standing by you makes all your successes more meaningful, and this ride called life a worthwhile experience.

Dismissing what Michaela deemed made-up words for Isabella's benefit, Antonio's voice spread the liquid warmth in her belly. Michaela slid her hand under her dress and traced her fingers along the edge of the silk that covered her. She raised the volume on the laptop and settled back, rewound and played.

"A loving, supportive woman sharing your life and dreams and standing by you makes all your successes more meaningful, and this ride called life a worthwhile experience," Antonio's voice rang.

"It does, *amore.* It does," Michaela said on a breathy exhale, slipping her fingers under her silk panties. She was close to orgasm. Antonio always had that effect on her.

Imagining Antonio piercing her, feeling him inside her as she often did, Michaela let her fingers glide through the moist heat. She pictured herself yielding beneath him and rising to meet him. Michaela pleaded with him not to stop.

"Faster, my darling, faster," she said, whispering his name and hearing hers on his lips.

She built up the pleasure and sent fabulous, shocking ripples through her body. Her moans were passionate and loud.

"You have magical fingers, *amore*. I'm ready. I'm ready, my love. Make it so I scream your name."

Her body arched when the orgasm burst into her system like lightning and thunder balled into one. Her fingers frenziedly worked to drive the next orgasm to erupt.

"Fill me, Antonio. Fill me with everything you are," she cried.

Michaela threw back her head. Her entire body shuddered as she cried Antonio's name like a reverent prayer when she came.

Michaela's face flushed, and she let herself catch her breath. There was no better touch than Antonio's, Michaela thought with a slaked smile.

Michaela's joy was short-lived when she caught sight of Isabella on the paused video, sitting next to Antonio, his hand wrapped around hers. The bitch spoiled everything, always had.

Michaela punched the enter key on the laptop and let the video play through to the end. She watched the family around the table, all smiles, happy, doing what loving families do.

Angry eyes flashing like two hot flares, Michaela picked up the glass of wine and whipped it at the white wall. Red splattered everywhere.

Michaela should have given Antonio that family, not Isabella. She, not Isabella, should sit beside Antonio and warm his bed. She should be at that table. The engagement came about because of her, and she was Toni's mother.

Isabella took her man and now took her daughter. The anger vibrated and pulsed inside Michaela's chest, and she rose to pace the apartment. Michaela's pace accelerated, as did her anger. She screamed at the top of her lungs.

After her third glass of wine, Michaela fished a cigarette from the crumpled pack she dug up between the sofa cushions. Firing up the cigarette, she breathed in deep and exhaled long.

Michaela wouldn't allow Isabella to play her for a fool again.

Michaela sat up and typed her response to Sheldon.

Hello Amore,

I, too, am craving the taste of you in my mouth, the feel of you inside me. I want you so badly that I just finished pleasuring myself with thoughts of you in my head. I screamed your name, wishing you were the one touching me.

I need you. I want you. I must see you.

I'm hopping on a plane tomorrow and will be there by dinnertime. Will you pick me up at the airport and arrange for my accommodation? Ideally, your downtown apartment would be the perfect meeting place for us. I want you in my bed often and for as long as you can get away from your wife.

I can't wait to see you, my lover boy.

Michaela

Michaela hit send.

That should get her free lodgings for the duration of her stay. Michaela had to have boots on the ground. She couldn't accomplish what she aimed to do an ocean away. She wouldn't allow Isabella to make a fool of her—again.

Sheldon Tanner saw Michaela's email at the ping on his phone and smiled. Sheldon had been expecting it.

Sheldon didn't know where Michaela's hatred for Isabella Farfalla stemmed from or why. What Sheldon knew was that the minute Michaela saw the video, her reaction would be swift.

No matter her reason, Michaela was on her way to Toronto. Sheldon would give her lodgings and financial and whatever support she wanted during her stay in exchange for great sex. Sheldon only wished Michaela wasn't so overly demanding or batshit crazy. Nothing came free in this life.

Sheldon hoped Michaela didn't ask him to have Isabella killed again. As much as Michaela dismissed the comment as a joke after she saw the shock on his face, Sheldon believed she meant it.

Batshit crazy Michaela was, but she was too good in bed to dismiss. The sacrifices a man made for great sex.

Sheldon typed his reply email.

I can't wait to see you. The apartment will be at your disposal for as long as you want. Rest on the plane because you'll need your energy when you get here.

Sheldon pressed send.

Chapter 9

AS MICHAELA'S PLANE skidded to a landing, she peeled her eyes out the window. The late afternoon sun shone in a clear blue sky, but traces of the earlier rain were everywhere. Puddles of water slowly evaporating dotted the tarmac. Beyond the runway, the rain-soaked grass gave off a green lushness.

After a two-hour boarding delay and the six-hour flight, Michaela was ready to set foot on land. She might have flown first class, but it wasn't the comfort of a private jet, which her daughter now had access to through Isabella's company.

Had Michaela flown private, she wouldn't have had to endure delays or go through the demeaning task of standing at a conveyor belt with coach travellers to claim her bags. Michaela wouldn't have to queue to go through passport check with ordinary folk.

Michaela piled the resentment onto the growing mountain of bitterness mounting for her selfish daughter, for privileged Isabella and her family.

After claiming her bags, Michaela went to the bathroom to wash the common off her. She freshened up her red lips and the bronze eyeshadow over the blue eyes. Michaela fluffed out her flowing blonde hair and unbuttoned the third button on her lime-green shirt to expose cleavage and the creamy swell of her taut breasts. Twisting and turning in front of the mirror, she checked her butt against the fitted Gucci Jeans. Pleased with what she saw, Michaela made her way to the arrivals gate.

Michaela immediately spotted Sheldon amongst the throng of people, towering over them and looking handsome. Sheldon wore his customary tan leather jacket against a sky-blue shirt, Levi jeans, and tan loafers. His short, dark, freshly trimmed hair crowned the beautiful, tanned face with smiling blue eyes. Under Sheldon's right eye, he had a horizontal one-inch scar, a souvenir from an angry husband who caught him clicking the camera from outside the motel window at him and his lover. Sheldon's nose was slightly crooked, a memento from the woman who swung her umbrella at him when he moved to prevent her from kidnapping her son.

Michaela guessed Sheldon to be in his mid-fifties. Michaela assumed this because asking Sheldon his age risked him asking hers. Age was a state of mind and not essential information. Michaela knew what needed to be known about Sheldon Tanner, which was that he enjoyed sex and liked to keep her happy when she fulfilled his fantasies. The simple mathematics of every relationship Michaela had.

Michaela smiled with all her warmth and waved to catch Sheldon's attention. "Hello, Lover-Boy."

"Hey, baby." Sheldon took her into a deep kiss. Michaela tasted the bourbon on his tongue and smelled it on his breath.

"You started partying without me."

"I had to do something with myself. I've been waiting for you for an hour, but it was worth the wait."

The eager, wanting look on Sheldon's face pleased Michaela. "You already horny for me, Lover-Boy?"

"I'm steel-hard for you right now, baby. Have been all day." Sheldon pressed himself against Michaela.

A wicked gleam filled Michaela's eyes. "Hmmm. Mr. Big is ready for me. I can't wait to please him and you."

"Christ! You drive me crazy, baby. I've been anticipating your arrival since you emailed me. I told my wife I'd be out of town on assignment all weekend."

She bit on her bottom lip. "Then, I'll fulfil your every need tonight, tomorrow and Sunday."

"Let's get this party started, baby. I have Cristal on ice at the apartment waiting for us."

Smiling, at the prospect of her weekend with Sheldon, Michaela linked her arm through. "Lead the way Lover-Boy."

A few days in bed with Sheldon should get her bank account topped, an indefinite stay at his apartment, and the investigative services she needed in the coming days.

Chapter 10

TONI CHECKED THE last email of the day on her laptop before clocking out and clicked it open. It was the Ming Project folder. Toni's lips curved into a smile, not because Margie, Carole, and Suzanne were turning the program over to her, but because it validated their and Bianca's trust in her. Slowly but surely, Toni was regaining her role in the company's hierarchy.

Toni read on. The document showed that Ming and her teammates had made excellent strides in the cutthroat male-dominated gaming world. They had progressed to the next level due to the Farfalla funding Toni secured for the team. Proof that all the girls needed was financial backing to advance through the ranks and prove their gaming skills. Now, they stood an excellent chance to win the year's tournament. Girls ruled even in the gaming world.

On top of their success, the team's rise to fame would play perfectly into the launch of the G@merwe@r clothing line projected for the end of the year. Toni had seen the preliminary sketches Lorenzo's team presented to Bianca and had no doubt it would generate the millions in sales Christian projected in his report.

Toni stood to make a generous bonus from the sales of G@merwe@r since Ming and her team came to Bianca's attention through her recommendation. But it wasn't about the money for Toni. It was about helping Ming and her team achieve their goal and the sense of accomplishment and recognition Toni got for a job well done. It was about the pride Toni felt for the first time.

Toni's busy day had her working through lunch, and the gnawing hunger that hit her became hard to ignore. It was seven p.m., and Toni decided to clock out for the day.

Toni packed the laptop in her briefcase. She'd finish reading the file at home. Toni collected her things and stopped by Bianca's office to let her know she was off for home.

Forty minutes later, Toni brought her Porsche to a stop on the driveway of her home. The lampposts around the circular driveway burned bright against the night. The house was dark, a reminder that Christian was away in New York on business, and tonight, she'd have to settle for a microwaved meal and an empty bed.

Toni closed the front door behind her and tossed her keys in the bowl on the foyer table. Toeing her pumps off, Toni made her way to the kitchen. A tall glass of wine and a bowl of the leftover lasagna Christian made a few days ago would hit the spot. Afterward, Toni would treat herself to a hot bubble bath before sliding into bed and calling Christian, if only to hear his voice. The second day of sliding into the empty bed made Toni crave Christian's company and warm body next to her.

Flicking the kitchen light on, Toni saw the woman sitting at the table. A chill settled in the room. She wore a sleeveless dress exposing toned arms. Her blonde hair spilled from beneath the wide-brimmed white hat to her shoulders. White pearls hung around her neck and ears, a gift from one of her many lovers.

Toni stopped and froze on the spot.

The emotionless gaze Michaela fixed on her daughter sent an icy shiver down Toni's spine.

Her office attire was professional and classy looking. Michaela could smell Farfalla's famous scent. Toni's once blonde hair, now a rich golden brown, spilled around a flawlessly made face.

"You look good. Glamorous. And this place is nice, luxurious. A far cry from your past dwelling." Michaela's gaze was level and steady as she looked at Toni. "It's just as you described it. That is when you were taking my calls."

Toni's gaze moved around the room, looking for her mother's accomplice. Michaela didn't get her hands dirty. "How did you get in here? How did you find me?"

"Those are the first questions you have for your mama after you've refused to take any of my calls for months?" Michaela stared hard at her daughter, compelling Toni's expression to soften considerably.

"Sorry. How are you, Mama?"

"That's better." She leaned back a little in her chair and rested her toned forearm on the back of her chair.

"Much better now that I've seen you, *amore*. You look radiant, and I like the new look."

Toni skimmed her hand through her hair. "I needed a change from…. I needed a change."

Michaela studied her daughter. She wore a five hundred dollar mauve, silk pants suit with gold buttons against a silk cream blouse. Toni embodied confidence and professionalism. The ruby and surrounding diamonds on her left hand threw a brilliant prism of light that caught Michaela's attention.

"Look at that positively marvellous ring. It's worth at least fifty thousand dollars. You figure he could do better with the type of money he has. Still, it's a conversation starter. Congratulation, *amore*." Michaela crossed her very impressive legs.

Toni slipped her hands into her pants pockets.

"Don't be modest, *amore*. You've arrived and should shout it from the rooftops. Marrying such a gorgeous specimen, and a filthy rich one, is quite the accomplishment."

"Christian will be home soon." Toni lied, hoping to get Michaela to leave.

"Did you forget he's in New York for a couple more days? Meeting with those highfalutin bankers from Wall Street takes time."

Toni simulated the piano-playing fingers against her thigh. Michaela smiled at the gesture. She was having the intended impact on her daughter.

Toni walked to the refrigerator, opened it, and picked up the bottle of Zinfandel. Uncorking it, she poured wine into a glass and tossed most of it back. Toni topped it up. Her mother always compelled the necessity for copious amounts of alcohol.

"Hopefully, he's the type of man to keep his hands and eyes to himself," Michaela said.

Toni's eyes narrowed, and her jaw set tightly. "Of course he will. We love each other." Toni drank.

"Love is a myth. It doesn't exist, not where men are involved. I'll take one of those," Michaela said when Toni didn't offer her a glass of wine. "Bring the bottle over."

Toni set the bottle and a glass before her mother and watched Michaela sip at her wine. "

It's not a myth. Our love is real," Toni said.

Michaela let out a deep chuckle. "Of course it is."

"No smoking in the house," Toni said when Michaela pulled out the cigarette pack and lighter from her Prada handbag.

"My apologies. God forbid I sully your grand home." Michaela dropped the cigarette pack and the lighter into her handbag. "How's your father?"

Toni gazed at Michaela with a blank expression, but Michaela could see the shock in her eyes.

Michaela smiled faintly. "You didn't think I knew you'd connected with him and lived in his home until you got engaged and moved with Christian to the opulent Mesi Villa?" Michaela toasted with her glass of wine. "You are living the dream."

Toni swallowed heavily, then went on more firmly. "Why did you not tell me about him?"

"Your father was a drunk who couldn't hold a job. All he had going for him was that he was good, no great, in bed, I'll give him that."

Toni winced. "He is very successful now. He has a beautiful family, a lovely wife, and home." *Funny how that came about when he left you.*

"I'm happy for him. I'm glad he managed to get over his alcoholism because he was a living nightmare. It's why I didn't tell you about him. I wanted to protect you from that."

"That is not how he tells his side of the story. Yes, Mama, he told me everything. Everything." Toni's fingers moved back and forth along the countertop, playing Moonlight Sonata.

"If he's told you everything, then there's nothing I can add because it seems you're going to believe him over anything the mother, who raised you, nursed you to health when sick, was the only parent by your bedside, says."

Toni's wine glass was nearly empty, and she refilled it. "Overly dramatic is your way."

Michaela gave Toni an arched look. The girl had a sharp tongue, but Michaela had no one to blame but herself. Toni was who she made her.

"I'm happy you found your father."

No, thanks to you.

"Tell me more about Joe. What type of business does he own? Is his home large? How successful is he?" Michaela enjoyed her wine and watched Toni.

Toni studied her mother intently and saw Michaela with more clarity. Michaela knew precisely what Joe did for a living. All this time, she had known of Joe's successes. Michaela knew of his family and where he lived.

Toni's eyes went hard. "Don't interfere with his life and family. I'm warning you, Mama." Toni was surprised to hear the stiffness in her voice, just as Michaela was.

Michaela responded with an unyielding look, and Toni felt its full weight. The uneasiness crept up her spine—for the second time.

Toni's eyes had an apology forming. "Please don't ruin this for me, Mama. You won't, will you?"

In the immeasurable silence that followed, Toni watched Michaela turn the glass in little circles on the table.

"No, I'm not, darling. I wouldn't jeopardize your good fortune," Michaela said.

Toni sighed a breath of relief. "Thank you, Mama."

Michaela paused and stared past Toni out the dark window. A moon cut in half shone brightly in a starry sky. The land that stretched far and wide, which Toni stood to own when she said I do to Christian, was misted with a haze of blue. Michaela wouldn't dare ruin things for her daughter. She had plans for Toni's inherited wealth.

"You've hit the mother lode with Christian, and I want in on it."

Toni's heart sank deep in her chest at the words. She would never be free of her mother's insatiable need for money and control of her.

"No, Mama. That is not going to happen."

"But, darling, I'm all alone. How am I to survive?" Michaela's eyes were drenched in feigned sadness.

Toni gave Michaela a frank and cagey stare out of blue eyes. "You are here and looking like your usual affluent self. It tells me you have found your next mark and used him well." Toni drank. "I do not want that life anymore. I do not want to steal, cheat, and lie anymore. I do not want to degrade myself by sleeping with disgusting old me for money. Never again. Do you hear me, Mama?" Toni's tone was defiant.

"I see." As quiet as Michaela's voice, it projected volumes. "You know what I'm capable of, *amore*." Michaela rose and took the last of her wine. "Don't make me go that route because you know I will."

"What are you planning to do, Mama? You said you were not going to ruin this for me."

"I wouldn't dream of it, but as I said, I want to share in your good fortune." Michaela set her empty glass on the table.

"Please do not do anything to hurt me, Mama. I beg you."

"I'll be in touch. And, *amore*, I'd keep this between us, or I'll be forced to tell Christian about everything. Everything."

"What does that mean?" Toni said quaveringly.

As silent as Michaela was, it projected volume.

"What are you going to tell Christian?"

A wide grin filled Michaela's face at the fear she saw in her daughter's eyes. "I doubt you've told your husband to be everything. Had you, he likely wouldn't be marrying you." Michaela walked out, leaving Toni staring after her.

Chapter 11

TONI SHUT THE door firmly behind her mother, listening for the reassuring click of the latch. She double-checked that every window was securely closed and locked, ensuring her home was safe and sound. Making her way throughout the house, Toni forced her mind to recall if she forgot to arm the alarm system that morning, but her mind was crowded with her mother's words, making it difficult to think clearly. Toni would ensure to set the alarm system on from here on.

Toni's nerves jumped; she bypassed the relaxing bath she was looking forward to. In her bedroom, Toni undressed, slipped into an oversized T-shirt, and collapsed in bed. Her mother could drain every ounce of energy out of her. Michaela could trigger a deep-seated hate in Toni for her she didn't know she possessed.

Michaela's words rolled through Toni's head, and too exhausted from her long day at the office, she found sleep impossible. Toni cushioned her head on the clasped hands behind her head and stared at the ceiling.

A secret could be a corrosive thing between two people, Toni told Christian and vowed to tell him everything. Toni had told Christian the truth about her ugly past but hadn't told him everything. And her mother knew precisely what Toni had held back from Christian.

Toni wanted to tell Christian everything, but she couldn't tell him about that part of her life. She just couldn't. Toni didn't bring it up out of deceit but because she couldn't bring herself to say the words.

Toni could kick herself for her lack of foresight and for not factoring in the possibility of her mother's impedance. Toni should have known better. Michaela Trevi was a resilient woman who would stop at nothing to get what she wanted, and what she wanted was control of Toni and her life.

How was Toni to tell Christian now what she conveniently omitted to reveal? Toni pondered. Telling Christian the truth would result in his distrust of her. Then there was Bianca. If Bianca found out, she would conclude Toni could be compromised—again.

Toni stood to lose everything: Christian, the trust she had painstakingly rebuilt with Bianca, the job she loved, and the family she came to think of as her own. Toni would lose the people who had gone out of their way to make her life whole. Toni would need to put distance between her and her father, brothers, and sisters because imposing Michaela's wrath on their lives wasn't an option.

Toni considered leaving, running away from everyone and everything she loved. She was tired of living alone, without a foundation or support system, with no sense of direction, but there was no option.

Toni's world felt undone.

Goddamn her mother for putting her in such a compromising situation.

Chapter 12

IN THE MORNING, Toni had the unfocused look that stemmed from sleeplessness, with her mind firmly preoccupied by her worries. Toni wondered how productive she would be at work and debated calling in sick.

After the third espresso, Toni's mind perked up, and she decided to keep her mind occupied with work and not focus on the misery that was her life was what she needed.

Looking troubled and bewildered, Toni remained strangely quiet throughout Bianca's meeting with Margie, Carole, and Suzanne to bring her up to date on the Ming Project.

Bianca looked the epitome of elegance in a black knee-length pencil dress. Her chestnut hair tied into a smooth ponytail underscored the face painted in muted tones, and the lips glossed pink. Bianca was proof that less was more.

"Do you have any questions for the ladies, Toni?"

Dropping her gaze, Toni shook her head. Her ash-brown hair swept over her shoulders, covered in the cream-coloured dress she wore.

Toni's impassive response to the turnover of the program she conceived set Bianca's mind dancing. Bianca looked at Toni, appraising her. Bianca considered wedding planning and work pressures were taking a toll on Toni. Toni's long work hours were likely catching up with her. But after more serious consideration, all roads led to Michaela.

"Thank you, ladies." Bianca capped her pen. "Please pass all the available information to Toni. She'll be taking the project over, full-on, as of today. I hope you will assist Toni by any means necessary."

"Of course we will, Bianca. You can count on us, Toni, for whatever you need," Suzanne offered in an overly eager tone that rang of insincerity.

Toni's mind was elsewhere, and she didn't react or respond.

"Toni appreciates it, ladies. If there's nothing else on the agenda, let's bring the meeting to a close," Bianca said, and everyone shut their laptops.

Toni's head bowed, she rose with Margie, Carole, and Suzanne and followed the women out of Bianca's office. Toni was halfway across the room when Bianca called her back to her desk.

"Bianca waved Toni to the guest chair. "You look tired, Toni."

Toni said nothing.

"I know you've been putting in a lot of hours and, as always, doing a great job. I want to know if you're all right with taking over the Ming Project full-on, Toni. If it's too much on your plate, I can get you help," Bianca said, hopefully getting Toni talking and opening up about what bothered her.

"No, it is not too much to handle, Bianca. I am pretty much caught up and will be able to devote the necessary time and effort to the project." Toni's gaze focused beyond Bianca, past the glass wall, giving a clear view of the blue lake under the spill of sunshine.

A handful of sailboats and two kayakers glided on calm water. To the west, the downtown core came into view. Mid-morning traffic crowded the road and pedestrians the sidewalks. The sun and blue sky reflected off the windows of the tall buildings. The siren from a fire truck was heard, although it was difficult to determine where the sound came from.

"Have you had a chance to read the entire file?" Bianca's words had Toni flicking her eyes toward her.

"Yes. I read it yesterday."

Bianca peered at Toni as she nervously tucked her hair behind her ear. "What do you think about the progress made?"

"They have done very well, better than I hoped. It will be good for sales of the G@merwe@r line," Toni said without the enthusiasm Bianca expected.

"Yes, it will. I anticipate doubling Christian's projected sales numbers within the first year."

"That is good news." Toni's voice was artificial and unalive.

"It is. Christian is often very conservative with his projections, but doubling numbers is an unexpected but welcomed news."

"It is."

Succinct, Bianca thought. "More than that, I'm pleased we could help the girls achieve their goal, and it's because of you they did. You should be proud of that, Toni."

"I am."

"You know that you stand to make a substantial bonus once the sales of G@merwe@r take off. You...."

Toni broke in peremptorily. "I do not want the money. I would like to give the money to the girls."

Bianca stared in surprise. "That's very generous, but it's not necessary, Toni. The company will continue to support them in their endeavour."

"I insist, Bianca. I do not want the money. It is better I do not...." Toni stopped and locked eyes with Bianca. "It is better I do not get the money."

Bianca noted Toni's piano-playing fingers on the arm of the chair. Bianca rose, rounded her desk, and eased her hip on the edge. "Are you all right, Toni?"

Toni's eyes cut away from Bianca. "I am. I just ... haven't been sleeping well. You know, with Christian away and being alone in that big house." Toni's fingers played faster at the lie.

"Why didn't you say so? You're welcome to stay at our place."

"No. I could not intrude on you and Lorenzo."

"No intrusion. We have enough room, and the girls and Romeo would love to have you for a sleepover." The long pause told Bianca that Toni was searching for the words to turn her down. Before Toni could say anything, Bianca said, "I won't take no for an answer. We'll clock out on time tonight and ride home together."

"But I don't have any clothes or...."

"You're my size, and I'm sure I can dig up an extra toothbrush. I'll call Nanny to let her know so she can get dinner for us and the guest room ready." Bianca pushed off the desk and smoothed the front of her dress. "Let's get back to work so we can leave on time."

"Okay, Bianca. Thank you." Toni rose and headed for the door.

Bianca's eyes followed Toni as she walked to the door with a clouded look. After dinner, Bianca planned to sit Toni down and find out what was bothering her. Bianca's gut told her whatever it was, she needed to nip it in the bud.

Chapter 13

TONI SAT RIGIDLY in the car's back seat beside Bianca as the chauffeur wound the car through the thronged streets. Toni's thoughtful eyes remained peeled out the car's window for the entire ride home. Not one word was spoken. The silence stretched, and Bianca gave Toni the needed space.

The moment the driver stopped the car in front of the house, an excited Serena opened the front door and Romeo followed her out and zoomed around the driveway barking. It lifted Toni's spirits—some.

"Look, Auntie Toni." Serena flashed a toothless grin. Serena's dark hair was tied into pigtails, and her cheeks and nose had a rosy glow from the summer sun. "And this is what the tooth fairy left under my pillow." Serena flashed the five-dollar bill she dug from her shorts pocket.

"That is a lot of money, *amore*." Toni released Serena from the tight embrace and delighted Romeo with head scratches. "I hope you are planning to invest wisely."

"If investing means buying, I plan to buy Romeo a bone." At that, Romeo barked, and his tail swished in excitement, prompting a giggle from Serena. "And with the rest, I plan to get myself a Nintendo Switch with a detachable joy con—a pink one. I like pink. And if I have leftover money, I want to buy a pony."

Toni's bemused eyebrows raised. "That is quite the list."

Serena crooked her finger, signalling Toni to bend to her level so she could whisper in her ear. "Uncle Chris told me he'd lend me the money if I needed some."

"What have I said about asking Uncle Chris for money?" Bianca bent down to kiss her daughter on the cheek.

"You weren't supposed to hear that, Mommy and I didn't ask. Uncle Chris offered." Serena followed Bianca and her mother into the house.

"Still, you shouldn't accept." Bianca set her briefcase and handbag on the foyer table.

Serena tucked the five-dollar bill into the pocket of her pink polo shirt. "But, Mommy, how am I supposed to afford a pony if I don't let Uncle Chris help."

Toni and Bianca stifled their amusement. "Lorenzo and I are working on teaching the girls about money management. Where's Rosanna, baby?"

"She's sun tanning by the pool with Leanne and Abbey." Serena rolled her big blue eyes. "And would like to be left alone by Romeo and me."

Putting her arm around the girl's shoulder, Toni said, "How about you and I take Romeo for a walk."

At the suggestion, Romeo ran enthusiastic zoomies around the foyer, down the hallway, and temporarily disappeared before reappearing and racing toward them.

Romeo's performance sent Serena into joyful giggles. "I think he's happy we're going out."

"I think so too. Is it okay with you, Bianca, if I take Serena and Romeo for a walk?" Toni asked

"Of course." Delaying the inevitable, Bianca thought. "Dinner won't be for another forty minutes. We're waiting for Lorenzo to get home. Would you like to change into comfortable clothes and trade heels for

comfortable flats, before going on your walk, Toni?"
Bianca said, and Toni nodded.

"Mommy says you're staying for a sleepover." Serena
glanced over her shoulder at Toni as they went up the
stairs to Bianca's bedroom.

"I am, *amore*."

"Can we have a tea party in my room later on? Rosie
says she's too old for tea parties anymore."

"Who is going to be there?" Toni asked.

"Peppa Pig and little Big Bird. Mommy says I can't
invite the big Big Bird because he won't fit in my room.
And Romeo, of course," Serena said when Romeo barked
from the top of the stairs.

"All delightful guests. I will attend." Toni followed
Bianca into the bedroom.

Serena ran in with Romeo, and together they jumped
on the bed. "You know it's a make-believe tea party.
Mommy says I can't have hot tea in my room."

Toni touched a finger to the tip of Serena's nose.
"Make-believe tea parties are the best, and I know yours
will be."

Serena felt a rush of pride, and her face turned happy.
"I wish you could stay here always, Auntie Toni. You and
I can hide away in my room and play together."

"Me too, *amore*. Me too." Toni's blue eyes swam in
sadness.

Chapter 14

TONI REMAINED ENGULFED in silence through dinner, and picked at her food. Now, sitting on the sofa in Bianca's study for an after-dinner cognac while Lorenzo spent quality time with the girls, Toni's thoughts were anywhere but there.

With her drink in hand, Bianca joined Toni on the sofa. "Earth to Toni," Bianca said, sensing her mind miles away.

"Hmm." Toni turned to Bianca when she heard her voice.

"I hope Serena wasn't too much of a bother," Bianca repeated.

Toni shook her head. "I enjoy spending time with Serena. She is a sweet girl. In the end, she invited Queen Elsa to the party, and Rosanna joined in."

A stunned surprise flashed on Bianca's face. "Rosanna joined in? You had to have had a hand in that."

"I explained to Rosanna how Serena looked up to her big sister and the influence she has on her."

"It would have been dismissed as nonsense if I'd said as much. Because I'm only their mother."

"We were all young and silly at one time. The main thing is Rosanna joined in and enjoyed the party, and Serena could not have been happier to have her big sister there." Toni rose and walked to the opened window to give Bianca her back when she felt her questioning eyes on her.

The aroma of lilac, lavender, and roses from the gardens in glorious bloom flowed into the room. One hundred yards out, beyond the glowing lamp posts spreading light along the driveway, the shapes and shadows of the night floated through the trees and over the land. Toni heard musically chirping crickets and saw four glowing eyes in the distance: foxes or raccoons.

"You have a way with kids, Toni." Bianca stretched her legs on the coffee table and crossed her bare feet at the ankles.

Bianca had changed from her office attire into slim jeans with a copper-brown tank top featuring a gold-knitted butterfly symbolizing the Farfalla logo.

"I love children. I would love a full house, and the girls make it easy to love them. You should be proud of them. They are both well-adjusted, funny, clever girls."

"Thank you, and I am, but you wouldn't say so if you lived with them," Bianca commented with a wink.

"You know Christian, and I will babysit the girls anytime you and Lorenzo need time to yourselves."

"You should be careful what you say. I may take you up on that offer often." Bianca watched Toni's eyes drown in thought.

"Christian loves children." Toni sat on the sofa again with her knees together and her hands folded on her lap.

"He does. He, too, would have a house full of them, but I think he'd settle for two. At least that's what Mom would like. No pressure." Bianca walked to the desk and reached into the top drawer for a scrunchie.

"Yes, lineage and carrying on the flawless legacy of the Farfalla and Sabatini name is important. Isn't it?" Reflectively, Toni twirled the stem of her nearly full cognac snifter.

Bianca finger-combed her hair into a ponytail and bound it with the black scrunchie. "It's not about lineage as much as being a grandmother because as far as sustaining the Farfalla and Sabatini names, they've already made their mark in the annals of history." Bianca set her feet back on the coffee table.

"Rosanna, as much as Serena, God help us, and your children will carry their legacy. Mom and Dad built the company through hard work, sweat, and dedication and believe your legacy is derived from your actions and the positive impact you make throughout your lifetime. 'Your surname is attached to your actions, good or bad. Better to be remembered for the good,' is what Dad always says."

Toni reflected on that. "Truer words have not been spoken."

Hearing the shame in Toni's voice, Bianca countered with, "No, Toni, that's not what I meant at all. You're misconstruing what I've said."

"I am the totality of my past actions. I cannot change that. It is who I am and what I bring with me."

Bianca leaned forward in her seat and intently looked Toni in the eye. "Who you were, Toni, past tense. You're not that person anymore. Now, you have a father who loves you and a stepmom who adores you. You have brothers and sisters and their extended families. You have Christian and us now. You're not that person anymore. You have a loving network of people who care for you and will protect you."

Toni swung her head to meet Bianca's eyes. "But I am that person, Bianca. In here." Toni pressed a finger to her temple. "I will always be that person. Mama will never let me forget it, and I will visit that on your family for as long as I am around."

Bianca's gaze lingered on Toni as the silence between them drifted. Toni's face held a lost expression, and the blue eyes idly stared into space, had a certain kind of disquiet. "What's this about, Toni? I sense this is more than a sense of morality or guilt."

Toni had told Bianca and Isabella everything about her life when they presented her with the DNA report proving her father's existence. Overwhelmed by the discovery after decades of speculation and grateful for filling the hole in her life, Toni bared her soul. Toni told them who she was and the shameful things she did to survive.

As shocked as Bianca and Isabella were by Toni's account, both assured her that her past was that—her past. Bianca and Isabella encouraged Toni to leave the past behind as they would.

Toni inclined her head when she felt the unexpected tears welling in her eyes. Drifting with her thoughts, Toni weighed her options.

Michaela was never going to give Toni peace. Michaela would always impose herself on Toni's life and those she loved. For as long as there was a breath in Michaela, she would inflict pain and chaos.

Toni felt the tightening feeling in her stomach Michaela forever brought on.

Bianca watched Toni with anxious energy, tapping her fingertips against her thighs. "Talk to me, Toni. You can tell me anything. I want to help you."

"I am leaving, Bianca," Toni divulged, making her mind up in that instant.

"What are you talking about?"

"I am leaving, and you must not tell anyone, least of all Christian. He will come looking for me. I will be gone by the time he comes home tomorrow."

"Calm down, Toni. Take a sip of cognac," Bianca said, and Toni tossed the drink back in one swallow.

"I must disappear from Christian's life, your life and the lives of the people I love." Toni buried her face in her hands. "It's the only way."

"The only way? Why do you feel you need to disappear?" Bianca's eyes rested on Toni.

"Because I must." Toni's throat tightened. "Just understand that I must."

"Let me help you, Toni." Bianca rested her hand on Toni's shoulder. "Isn't it time to find inner peace? It's not that hard to come by if you open up."

Brushing away her tears, Toni met Bianca's eyes. Toni saw compassion and sympathy in Bianca's eyes, and her composure started to fray. "It is my mother. She was waiting for me in the kitchen when I arrived home last night."

Sitting stiffly in her seat, Bianca shook her head in disbelief. "She broke into your house?"

"I do not know how she got in. She was waiting for me at the kitchen table."

Bianca shelved how Michaela got past the state-of-the-art alarm system and into the house for now. "What did she want, Toni?"

"What she always wants."

"Money," Bianca said knowingly.

"And control of me. Our relationship is not rooted in love but in what she can get from me. I will never be free of her." Toni angrily dragged a hand through her hair. "I do not know what made me think I could be." Toni's stomach muscles clenched, and she rose to pace the room. "I cannot bring this cauldron of chaos that is my life into Christian or your life. She will not stop there. She will poison Papa's life and everyone in it out of jealousy and greed. It's what she does. Do you understand why I must leave? Go far away from everyone."

Bianca heard the tears in Toni's voice. She put a protective sisterly arm around Toni's shoulder. "You're not going anywhere because I won't allow Michaela to touch or influence your life anymore. Christian and Mom won't allow it either. If she wants money, we'll give it to her."

"I cannot let you do that. Besides, I told Mama I would give her my work earnings."

"You can and will. The question is, will it be enough to leave you alone?" Toni sat motionless, saying nothing. "I didn't think so, but it's a start until we figure out how to extract you from Michaela's life. You'll get a substantial raise to ensure she gets off your back."

Toni cleared her throat to disguise the tears in her voice. "No, Bianca. You cannot do that. This is my problem."

"I can and will. I know it's what Mom would want. Mom would want to protect you, and I want to do that for you and Christian. And, Toni, this is *our* problem now. Family takes care of family."

Toni's tears came in sobs.

Chapter 15

TONI SLEPT SOUNDLY that night.

Bianca's offer to double Toni's salary to pacify Michaela eased the many thoughts crowding her head. The nagging worry of how to deal with Michaela lifted.

Waking to the sound of pattering rain against the roof, Toni blinked sleep out of her eyes. Sitting in the king-size bed covered in sea-blue Egyptian cotton and piled with down pillows, Toni looked out the window. The rain washed over the glass panes from a thunderous sky, beaded, and slid down like cascading waterfalls.

Toni rested her chin on her knees and reevaluated the plan she weaved to solve the dilemma Michaela had laid on her lap.

Toni hated to deceive Bianca, but it was a necessary evil. Toni had been through much in her short life but persevered because she was a survivor. Toni had survived the array of questionable scenarios her mother forced on her that would suffocate most, and she would survive Michaela's latest attack.

Warm colours, blues and browns dominated the room's decor. The floors were dark wood, and the walls were blue.

Toni turned on the flat screen above the marble fireplace and tuned it to the weather channel. The meteorologist reported the rain would end later in the morning, and the sun would shine on a warm day. Toni was glad she wouldn't drive to work this morning but hitch a ride with Bianca.

The first thing Toni intended to do was open a bank account under her name—one Christian knew nothing about. Bianca's offer to double Toni's salary made depositing her regular pay to her joint account possible. The remaining money Toni planned to use to pay her mother. Christian would be none the wiser about the payments or Michaela's appearance, and Bianca promised not to say anything. There would be no need for explanations.

Toni couldn't predict what else her mother planned to bribe her with or do to her, but no doubt she would. It was how Michaela worked.

As long as Michaela had money flowing into her account, Toni's secret would remain hidden. And Toni would make sure she kept the money flowing to her mother. No one would know about Angelica. No one.

Toni thought of Angelica often, and today was no exception as she slid into the past and brought it all back.

Angelica was seventeen years old. She was the spitting image of her mother. She had blue eyes and strawberry-blonde hair and was as brilliant as her father, Henry Morgan, a high-profile criminal lawyer. Angelica lived the best life with Henry, the type Toni could never have offered her.

Henry Morgan was three times Toni's age when their three-month affair led to her pregnancy. When Toni told Henry she was pregnant, he offered her one hundred thousand dollars to turn the baby over and disappear.

Toni turned Henry's offer down.

"Turning over my baby to your barren thirty-five-year-old wife will cost you two hundred and fifty thousand dollars, Henry. That will get you the baby and my silence. Think about it, Henry. Kill two birds with one simple payment to make your Barbie doll wife happy." Toni took the cigarette from Henry's fingers and drew on it.

Henry didn't flinch at Toni's demand. The legal papers were drawn and signed, and the transaction was made the second Toni gave birth. Toni didn't hold or look at her baby. It was for the best.

The knock at the door broke the threads of her thoughts, and she shook off the memory.

Serena opened the door a couple of inches and poked her head into the room. "Auntie Toni, can Romeo and me come in?"

"Romeo and I, and sure you can, *amore*."

Serena pushed the door open, and the dog and girl ran into the room and jumped on the bed. "Nanny says to get downstairs in thirty minutes for breakfast. She's making chocolate chip pancakes. They're my favourite. If you don't like them, I can tell her to make you something else. Rosie doesn't like them. They're fattening, she says. Do you like chocolate chip pancakes, Auntie Toni?"

Toni pushed off the bed and reached for the lavender silk robe. "If you like them, I love them."

Serena grinned. "I told you, Romeo, that she liked them." Serena leaped off the bed and gestured for Romeo to follow her. "Come on, let's go tell Nanny."

"Will you let Bianca know I need clothes for work?" Toni poked her head out of the bathroom. A cloud of steam haloed her. "I cannot go to work in my underwear. I will traumatize everyone there."

"What does trau … trau … that word mean?"

"Scare them dead."

Serena made a little snorting giggle. "Okay, Auntie Toni, I'll let her know."

Thirty minutes later, showered and dressed, Toni walked into the kitchen. She had on a peach blouse and black ankle-high pants with black pumps. Her thick black hair gleamed and fountained down to her shoulders.

Toni was ready for the day ahead.

Chapter 16

KEEPING BUSY, NOT that it took much effort when you worked for Bianca, took Toni's mind off her worries. It kept Toni's mind off Angelica.

Toni had sold her child, and she was no more her mother than Angelica was her daughter. Angelica was a Winston, not a Trevi. The clause Toni asked Henry to add to the contract stating Angelica was never to find out she was adopted ensured it remained that way. The life Henry and his wife gave Angelica was the life she deserved and would only know.

Toni didn't need Angelica to appear in her life with a sense of curiosity and inject unnecessary turmoil. Christian was the best thing to happen in her life, and Toni wasn't about to give it up for a girl she didn't know.

Toni organized Bianca's day and attended meetings with her to take minutes. Toni addressed dozens of emails and telephone calls and drafted reports. Keeping busy kept her mind busy. Before she knew it, the clock read six p.m.

Toni cleared her desk with a big smile and locked all pertinent documents away. Toni shut down her laptop but didn't pack it in her briefcase. Tonight, Christian was due home, and all would be right with the world again.

Toni stopped off at the supermarket and picked up a couple of steaks. Toni wasn't a cook, but she could handle sautéing meat in butter and olive oil with a sprig of rosemary and crushed garlic, as she watched Christian often do.

Toni bought a premade Greek salad and a bottle of the best merlot to pair with the steaks. A red velvet cake, Christian's favourite, was what Toni decided on for dessert.

The steaks were resting. The table was made, and the flames of two candles on silver holders burned straight and yellow. The air was scented with sautéed garlic and the sweet smell of the roses Toni set in the crystal vase at the centre of the table.

Toni was halfway up the stairs when the door swung open, and Christian walked into the foyer with a carry-on in one hand and a briefcase in the other. His jeans had knife-edged creases, and the white shirt clung to the impressive breadth of shoulders and sinewy arms. His dark hair was attractively tousled.

Christian slid the sunglasses off his face. His smile lit up the room and filled it with oxygen. Christian saw the beautiful face he missed waking up to and turned radiant with a smile. Before Christian could say anything, Toni lunged at him and took his mouth into a deep kiss.

Christian responded by wrapping his arms tightly around her waist. Pulling her close, he covered her mouth with his. "I've missed you."

"I have missed you more. In here," Toni pointed to her heart, "and in bed."

Toni's mouth on his was his. The feeling of need was potent, and Christian felt the strong spear of lust shoot to his groin.

"I've thought of nothing else." His fingers worked their way down to the buttons on her blouse.

"I have steaks resting in the kitchen."

"They can wait." He unbuttoned another button.

She skated a finger over his chest. "They will get cold." Her touch electrified his skin.

"We can microwave them." He slid his hand under her shirt to fondle her breasts.

Heat balled in her stomach, and she let out a long, breathless sigh. "You hate microwaved food."

"I'd eat the bottom of my shoe if I could take you here on this foyer, maybe the stairs, now."

She held her serious gaze on him for a moment. "Romantic."

"I can't be romantic when my hormones are wreaking havoc on my brain. I promise to be romantic later."

"Okay. If you promise." She tore her shirt and pants off. "Let us do it on the foyer and stairs."

Instant heat and need burst through him when he saw the red lace thong and bra against her creamy skin. "Is that new?"

"A gift from your sister."

"Jesus. You didn't have to tell me that."

She kept her gaze on his face. "Do not tell me you have gone soft on me."

Grinning, he shed his clothes. He was hard and ready for her. "It would take a lot more than the mention of my sister to turn me off you." Pulsing with heat and barely controlled, with the roughness of a ravenous bear, he pinned her against the wall. "I'm sorry, but no foreplay. I want you so badly I need to take you now," he said and drove himself into her hard and deep.

Riding on the thrill, she let out an orgasmic moan. "I have no problem with that." She tightened her legs around his waist and met him stroke for stroke until he built the pressure in her and him that sent shocking ripples through their bodies.

Twenty minutes later, he made love to her on the stairs. Christian took Toni on the kitchen table when she started to serve the microwaved heated steaks.

The kitchen table wasn't to be used to eat microwaved foods.

Chapter 17

SUNLIGHT POURED THROUGH the window, piercing Christian's sleep. He opened his eyes to see Toni propped on her elbow, gazing at him.

"We did not close the blinds last night," Toni said.

"We were too busy to think about inconsequential things like that." Christian's mouth tipped up at the corners.

"You look tired, *amore*."

Christian studied Toni's face. "How do you not? We barely got three hours of sleep."

Toni's eyes crinkled. "I am tired. You drained me of all my energy. I just hide it well."

That made him grin as pride rushed into him.

"Maybe you should take the day off to recuperate. I must get ready for work." Toni pushed off the bed.

Christian reached for Toni's hand when she started toward the bathroom. "Are you insinuating I'm old? Because that's not what you said last night."

Toni looked at him with a slow, curving lip. "I am not saying that at all. Last night proved you are anything but old. I am saying that you have been away and returned to only a few hours of sleep. That could take a toll on anyone. You should rest before you go to work today."

Christian's brow shot up. "Good save."

"Thank you. I am learning the art of the quick retort from Bianca."

"Yes, well, no one better to teach the art of quick retort than my sister. Anyway, I have too much to do. Being away has set me back days at work. But a long hot shower with you will pump me up for the day ahead."

With a half-laugh, Toni held out her hand for his. "Well, chop, chop, mister. I must shower to get ready for work."

Christian bolted to his feet. "Yes, ma'am."

Halfway to the en-suite bathroom, Toni slanted a look over her shoulder. "This time, I want foreplay and a more creative way to please me."

"I can make that happen."

Christian's hair curled with dampness from the shower when he walked into the smells of freshly brewed coffee and toasted cinnamon raisin bagels in the kitchen. Christian wore jeans and a white silk shirt. His cell phone was wedged between his cheek and neck as he rolled his sleeves to the elbows.

"Yes, please," Christian said when Toni waved the coffee cup in his direction.

Christian scraped one of the four stools, pushed against the kitchen island and sat. Toni brought a steaming cup of black coffee, a plate of toasted bagels, butter, jam, and a napkin.

"Yes, Bianca, I'll be in this morning. It's not like I need to rest up from my trip where I managed to secure the five hundred million dollar loan you wanted from the New York bankers for our American operation. You're welcome," Christian said to empty air when Bianca hung up. "That woman needs to chill some."

"She is under a lot of pressure at work." Toni buttered a bagel and added a strawberry jam layer before handing it to Christian.

"Aren't we all?" Christian took a bite of the bagel and chased it with black coffee. "Why didn't you tell me you spent the night at her place?"

The coffee cup she held in both hands stopped midway to her mouth. "Why would that come up in conversation?"

Toni wore a fitted white jacket with thin black lapels against a black shirt and white pants. Her blow-dried hair flowed in waves around her perfectly made-up face, with lips traced in glossy pink.

"It didn't. Serena answered her mother's phone and mentioned it after asking me if I was still willing to lend her money to buy a pony." Christian slathered a thicker layer of jam on his bagel.

"Bianca and Lorenzo are trying to teach Serena money management, and you are not helping by offering her money to buy a pony." Toni took a small, careful bite from her buttered bagel to not smudge her painted lips.

"It's a loan with a ten percent interest rate. I, too, am trying to teach Serena money management." Christian drank the last of his coffee.

"That is highway stealing." Toni watched him cross to the coffee pot on the hot plate and refill his cup.

"You mean highway robbery, and it's realistic financing. Finance is highway robbery for the average layperson. For the knowledgeable, it's a means to create wealth. I'm teaching Serena the latter."

Toni waved down the offer for a coffee refill. "You are a good uncle."

"The best." Christian walked to her, glided his lips over hers, and tasted the strawberry-flavoured gloss on her lips. "And you still haven't told me why you slept at Bianca's place."

"I was not sleeping well alone in this big house. Bianca picked up on it and invited, well more insisted, I should stay at their place."

Christian returned the pot to the burner and sipped on his coffee. "I guess sometimes it's a good thing she's always hard-wired to hone in on things. I'm sorry I left you alone."

"You do not need to apologize for doing your job. Besides, I had a wonderful time at Bianca's house. Serena invited me to a tea party with Peppa Pig, Queen Elsa, Rosanna, and Romeo."

"Good to hear. I probe because I was concerned after receiving an alert from the alarm company on Thursday night advising that the code had been entered wrongly twice."

Toni paused and stared at Christian for a prolonged moment as she put it together. Thursday night was when she found her mother in her kitchen. Toni had alarmed the system that morning. Her mother disarmed it. Toni wondered who Michaela's culprit was. Her mother wasn't savvy enough to crack the alarm passcode alone. Toni's mind raced, forming the lie she was to tell Christian.

"You told me everything was fine when I spoke to you, but now I find out you went to stay at Bianca's, which worried me."

"I am sorry. You know how useless I am with that alarm system. I will get used to it eventually. I should have told you, but I did not want to worry you." The lie flowed from Toni's mouth.

"No worries. I'm just glad you're okay, and you will get used to the alarm system soon enough. This weekend, we'll practice arming and disarming it. If worse comes to worst, I'll have the tech people from work install cameras throughout the property to make you feel safer when I'm away."

"No," Toni swiftly said, her eyes sliding away from Christian. "Umm, what I mean is you do not need to do that. The alarm already makes me anxious enough. More security will only make me more jittery."

Christian saw Michaela on camera, so stalking their home wasn't an option. Toni had to make sure of that.

"It's why I didn't want them installed. But the moment you feel you need them, you tell me. I want you to feel safe when I'm away on business." Christian bit into the last of his second bagel.

"I do feel safe." Toni reached into the dishwasher for their travel mugs and filled them with the remaining coffee in the pot. "I have to get used to staying alone when you travel, and if it comes down to feeling lonely, I will try to get invited to one of Serena's celebrity-studded tea parties."

Christian's eyes lit with laughter. "That's a good backup plan. Now, let's get packed up for work. Don't want to get the dragon lady coming at us for tardiness."

Part II

The Middle

The potential for loss is what makes things valuable.

—M.L. Lexi

Chapter 18

TONI SAT AT the conference table and dialled Ming's number. Ming's beaming smile came at Toni over her laptop screen. Ming wore a red sweatshirt and a matching ribbed knit beanie. Beneath the hat, straight strands of ebony-black hair framed her youthful face. Her bangs sat symmetrically above the equally dark eyes. On the wall behind her hung a ferocious female warrior waving a laser at her enemy.

"Hey, girl, you look sick, and your hair change is dope," Ming said.

"Thank you?" Toni's voice had the inflection of the perplexed when she couldn't decipher what Ming said.

Ming, a professional video gamer, spoke the gaming lexicon, but most of the time, Toni had no idea what she said.

"What she means is you look good." Xia appeared over her daughter's right shoulder to clarify.

Xia was the replica of Ming thirty years into the future. Xia wore her black hair in a loose ponytail, wisps of hair scattered over her face. She wore a black sweater over her jeans, and her face, like her daughter, had no traces of makeup.

"It's sick, Ma, not just good, is what I said." Ming rolled her eyes slightly upward.

"Yes, of course. Sick it is." Xia patted her eighteen-year-old daughter's head. "*Ni hao*, Toni, and my daughter is most right."

"Hello, back. You both look sick," Toni said with a smile.

"I know you lie. I am not as glamorous as you, but thank you." Xia raised her hands to tuck the loose strands of hair behind her ear. "And I must say congratulations. Ming tells me you are engaged."

"I am. Thank you."

"Her man is most sick looking, Ma," Ming jumped in to say.

"Yes, he is a very handsome, sexy man. I have seen pictures of him. He earned the most desirable bachelor title fair and square." Xia gazed at Toni through the video link with a mischievous expression. "You are back at work and will manage the project again, Toni?" Xia watched her daughter, with a laser-focused concentration on her face, expertly manoeuvre the joystick she picked up.

"I am back to work, and yes, I got the program assigned back to me a couple of days ago. I apologize for not calling sooner, but catching up has taken time. Anyway, I am calling now, and I wanted to say hello and tell you that your next installment payment is being processed."

Too focused on her game, Ming responded succinctly, "Um-hmm."

"What she means to say is thank you, Toni, for everything you have done for me. For all of your support," Xia slapped her daughter on the back of the head.

"Hey, was that necessary? Toni knows how grateful the girls and I are." Ming straightened her beanie. "We are so grateful we finna to promote the shit out of the G@merwe@r line day one."

Toni and Xia's brows furrowed.

"What have I said about speaking that way?" Xia slapped her daughter on the head again.

Toni watched mother and daughter launch into an animated argument in Mandarin. Hands flailed in the air, and emotions ran high, but Toni could see it wasn't in an adverse manner but radiant with tenderness and love. Toni envied them. She never had anything but cold, impassive interactions with her mother.

"Ladies. Ladies, please," Toni said and got their attention. "Xia, translate what Ming said, please."

"She says she and the girls are grateful, and in return, they are working out and making themselves, you know, more presentable to promote the G@merwe@r line the moment it is launched." Xia exhaled a breath. "I have been around the girls too long."

Ming raised the horned hand sign. "We gotchoo, Toni."

"She says they have your back," Xia said after a thoughtful pause to formulate the right words for Toni to understand. "I have definitely spent too much time with the girls. Anyway, I would like to say how grateful I am for helping Ming, Toni." Xia cozied up on the chair next to Ming. "Since you financially help Ming, I have been able to afford to travel with the girls and keep a close eye on them. You know they are still young to travel the world alone."

"Ma, I'm nineteen. Shit. I be sigma adulting on my own." Ming tsked at her mother.

Xia responded with a narrowed-eye look and said something in Mandarin that made Ming slump in her chair.

Toni gave Xia her warmest smile. "I am glad I could help. Do you mind if your mom goes with you to the tournaments, Ming?"

Ming pursed her lips slightly and nodded. "I wanted an open crib. You know parental units cramp your style."

Toni typed "open crib" into Google and discovered it meant living independently without parents. "Well, Bianca is pleased with the results, and the investment has helped you. She is happy to continue her support, but you must ensure you depict a positive, wholesome image. Xia being there with you does that. Do you understand, Ming?"

Ming blew a breath between her lips and sat back in her chair. "Yeah, yeah. Margie already gave me the four-one-one."

"Margie has already told her that." Xia clarified when Toni got the confused line between her eyebrows.

"Good, I'm glad she has," Toni said.

Ming caught something strange in Toni's voice. She leaned into the screen and looked directly at Toni. "Are you and Margie still not getty?"

"You and Margie still not get together," Xian decoded.

The silence that drifted for a while said it all.

"Let me give them the four-one-one, Toni, so u can be sigma with Margie and all."

Xia rolled her eyes. "She wishes to speak to Margie to tell her what was done to you. If Margie and everyone knew, they would be cool again. Not hate you, Toni."

Toni wished she could have told Margie, Carole, and Suzanne the whole story about the reason for her sudden departure from the company.

"They don't hate me. They are willing to work with me," Toni said.

"But you sense they think you're sus," Ming said.

"They don't fully trust you," Xia translated.

"Trust needs to be earned. When they are ready, they will." Toni said. "And we agreed never to speak about the extent of our internet involvement regarding Bob Klein and my mother."

"True that. I blank ya and my mind," said Ming.

"She says…."

Toni cut Xia off. "I got that. Now, give me a quick update on what has been happening in the past few months to update my files."

Chapter 19

DRAWING THE CALL with Ming and Xia to a close, Toni shut down her laptop and walked to her desk with a smile.

Ming was more focused on defeating her male counterparts than the two million dollar prize for first place. Ming and her team were on a mission to dominate the annual esports competition and prove women were as good as men.

Ming's motto was: Female gamers might be in the minority, but we are as good as any male player.

Toni couldn't be more proud of Ming and her teammates. Toni couldn't be more pleased that she had a hand in making their dream possible.

Toni's smile widened when she envisioned Ming getting in her competitor's face and yelling, "Get rekt, noob!"

Back at her desk, the clatter of office life was all around Toni. Ringing telephones squealed, photocopiers buzzed, and keyboards cluttered under typing hands. There was the buzz of staff conversation over work issues, their lives, or office gossip.

Toni picked up the ringing telephone. "Bianca Sabatini's office, how may I help you?" Toni said in her melodic Italian cadence.

"Hello, daughter of mine."

The merriment left Toni's face when she heard Michaela's voice. Toni's fingers tightened around the telephone's handset.

"What do you want, Mama?" Toni whispered, her gaze sweeping the room to ensure no one was listening.

"Is that any way to talk to the woman who gave you life?"

"I am very busy. What do you want, Mama?" Toni said briskly.

"Yes, the professional working woman. You know you're only a gopher, a lapdog for the mighty Farfallas. Bianca's in particular."

Demeaning Toni's accomplishments was Michaela's specialty.

Toni drew all the strength she had and filtered it to her voice. "I am going to hang up." The air of authority in Toni's voice took Michaela aback.

When Michaela found her voice, she said, "I haven't heard from you since our conversation at your place." Michaela stretched out on the buttery soft leather of the long, brown sofa, wearing nothing but a silk kimono.

Comfort and luxury were Sheldon's style, and it was all around Michaela in the loft-style apartment. Long leather sofas, matching chairs, mahogany tables, and the Persian rugs spread atop grey-streaked marble floors reflected who Sheldon was, and Michaela lavished in it.

The walls were cinder-block grey, and the art was colourful and priceless bold expressionism. The kitchen, dining room, and living room were one ample space fronted with ceiling-to-floor glass with a panorama of the city. At the top of the floating wrought-iron staircase were three spacious bedrooms.

"For your information, our conversations are taped," Toni informed her mother.

"To 'ensure the quality of customer service,'" Michaela caricatured the scripted, mechanical responses from telephone operators to convey interest that didn't exist. "So I'm right when I say that all you are is a customer service rep, a gopher, even though you're marrying into the family. You'd think they would appoint you to a vital role in the company. Fucking Farfallas never change."

Toni's nagging anxiety triggered her fingers to move back and forth along the desktop. "This so-called customer service job is what will get you a comfortable monthly allowance. I have already made the first transfer to your account, and you will receive electronic transfers bi-monthly." Toni's voice was hard as stone.

"Thank you, *amore*. I'll check the account to see if the amount satisfies my needs." Michaela's sanctimonious tone grated on Toni's nerves.

"It should be sufficient and will have to do. I am giving you my entire paycheque." Toni's voice punched like a tight fist.

Recognizing the anger in Toni's tone, a thin smile crossed Michaela's lips. "Darling, are you forgetting you are marrying one of the richest men in the country? He has unlimited funds, and my sources tell me you are now managing a twelve-million-dollar account, which you have complete access to. I believe it's called the Ming Project, which you brought about. A prouder mama I couldn't be."

Toni went cold from head to toe.

The silence hung momentarily as Toni reflected on the comment. Michaela knew about the project, its value, and her access to it. Countless questions leaped into Toni's mind. Several answers jumped at Toni, and all rounded back to the same one. After checking her home for listening devices and finding none—Michaela was too smart not to presume Toni wouldn't sweep her house after her visit—it was safe to conclude the enemy was within. The leaked information came from inside the company.

Toni's eyes scanned the room. She wouldn't put it past Michaela to bribe any of the thousands of employees working for Bianca for the information to use against her. Toni watched Margie, Carole, and Suzanne, who she presumed held a grudge against her, walk past her desk as they headed toward the conference room. Toni watched Thomas, Stephen, Dante, and Trent as if she could see through them. They were easy targets for Michaela and could, without effort, be manipulated into falling under her charming spell. It could be any of them or many others.

Toni felt trapped between desperation and hopelessness.

"I am giving you what you want. Stop interfering with my work life and manipulating the people I work with. I am warning you, Mama. Stop prying into my life, Christian's, and his family's. They are now my family," Toni said to drive the dagger into her mother's back.

Michaela laughed bitterly. "I am your family, and you know better than to threaten your mama, your flesh and blood." Michaela hung up before Toni could respond.

Chapter 20

TONI TOOK A break from her work for the first time that day. Her elbows were on the desk, and Toni held her coffee cup in both hands. Sipping cold coffee, she aimed her eyes out the window. The sun shone brightly in a stunning blue summer sky. The lake beneath it was a continuation of the pastel blue sky. Sailboats skimmed over the lake's calm waters.

Toni wished her racing mind would reflect the tranquil scene outside her window.

The conversation with her mother left Toni unsettled and as edgy as Michaela intended. Michaela thrived on the chaos and the anguish she inflicted on people's lives. Unsettling and controlling peoples' lives was a sport for Michaela, and Toni was no exception.

As long as Michaela remained in Toni's life, she would find no inner peace.

Toni checked the time. It was five p.m. Toni did the math. Six hours ahead would put the time at eleven in Milan. Her father would have returned from his nightly stroll with Francesca and was in his home office catching up on emails before bed. Toni clicked her laptop and dialled her father's number. A brief conversation with Joe would give Toni the inner peace she needed.

Joe Smith answered on the first ring. Joe looked polished and handsome in a grey cashmere sweater against a cobalt shirt opened at the collar. His hair was impeccably styled, and his dark eyes shone confidently behind the black-rimmed glasses. The wall-to-ceiling bookcase, filled with books and an array of eclectic art, served as the backdrop.

Joe gave Toni the special smile she felt he reserved for only her. "Hi, honey, it's nice to hear from you."

"Hello, Papa, how are you?" Toni said in the calmest voice she could muster. "I am not disturbing you, am I? I am not calling too late."

"You could never disturb me. How are you? How is your new job? How's Christian? Is he treating you well? He better be." Joe's voice was joyful, richly animated, with overtones of interest in her life.

"I am good. Christian treats me like a queen. The job is great. Very busy, but I like it that way," Toni's laughter rang out with joy, yet the worry in her eyes caught Joe's attention.

"Are you sure you're all right, *amore*?"

"Yes, everything is good. I wanted to hear your voice. How is Francesca?" Toni asked to shift the topic from her.

"I think you'd know the answer to that better than me. You video chat with Francesca and the girls more often than I see them."

"Well, yes, we do talk often, but you know the wedding is only four months away, and there is a lot of planning to do, or so I am frequently reminded." Toni turned and mouthed to Emily, "Have a good evening," when she walked past her desk on her way out the door.

"Listening to Isabella, Bianca, Francesca, Aurora, Mia, and you burn the video chat lines tells me the planning is in good hands. Sometimes, I think generals would be smart to leave the strategic planning of war to women," Joe remarked, and Toni smiled.

"I must agree with you," Toni said, and Joe could hear the unhappiness in Toni's voice.

"Everything all right, Toni?"

"Yes. Yes, everything is fine." Toni felt Joe's gaze on her. It was penetrating and made her nervous. Toni moved her fingers back and forth along the desktop.

The nervous, rapid playing and the tenseness in Toni's voice indicated one thing to Joe. "Has your mother reached out to you, Toni?"

"No, no, no. Why would you say that?" Her response was brisk. Too brisk.

Joe looked at his daughter steadily. Her nervousness and tense shoulders pressed down on Joe's chest. Joe's resentment for Michaela grew stronger than it ever had. Michaela was hurting *his* daughter.

"Because I'm your father and because I endured your mother's wrath for long enough to be familiar with the anxious voice you're trying to conceal. And because your fingers are about to etch a deep groove on the desk."

Toni slid her hands off the desk and tucked them under her legs to prevent further tapping. "It has just been a long workday. Between work and wedding planning, I am a little stressed." Hearing the two voices, Toni looked over her laptop and waved at Sam and Frank as they made their way out the door for the night.

"Um-hmm. Are you sure that's what it is, Toni? You know you can talk to me about anything." Joe poured himself a whiskey and sent part of it streaming down his throat.

"I know I can. I called because we have not spoken in a few days and wanted to say hello."

Joe paused for a moment and took a close look at his daughter. The tense shoulders and the troubled eyes she was trying to mask with a smile told Joe there was more to the call. Joe might have shed Michaela from his life long ago, but he knew the look on Toni's face well. Joe had felt the same distress and tension Toni felt—too often. But Joe didn't press Toni. Francesca had taught him patience was a virtue when decrypting the female thought process. Toni would tell him what was on her mind when she was ready.

"I'm only going to say one thing. If your mother…." Joe raised a finger to silence Toni. "No interruption while I say this, please. I want you to tell me if Michaela is the reason for your anxiousness. I'm here to protect you, Toni. I will do whatever is necessary to get her out of your life. The only way you will be filled with the peace you deserve is to get rid of her. You know I'm right."

Toni silently stared at Joe, biting on her bottom lip.

"I want your life filled with joy, love, and happiness. I know Christian would agree with me. Anyway, I'm glad you called because I'd like to submit a complaint." Joe settled back in his chair and sipped on his whiskey.

Toni shrugged. "A complaint? What about?"

"You know I'd do anything for you, *amore*." Joe tapped his pinky ring finger against his glass.

"I do."

"But having to wear tails at this wedding of yours is an issue for me. You know I'm a handsome devil, but looking like a penguin is a bridge too far to cross." Joe made a disagreeable face, and Toni broke into a smile of innocent pleasure that warmed him.

"You are complaining to the wrong person. I am only the bride. I have no say in any part of my wedding. You must submit your complaint in writing, in triplicate, to the wedding committee."

"I've made my thoughts clear to the committee, and they pfft me."

Toni's shoulders raised and fell as her mouth lifted at one corner. "I wanted a small church wedding with family and a few friends. I believe the guest list is up to three hundred."

Joe sank back in his chair. "Don't you think I know that? My accountant is having a coronary with the number of invoices he's getting," Joe said with a warm smile.

Feeling more upbeat after their exchange, Toni spoke to Joe for another thirty minutes. The conversation was about nothing of consequence, but Toni's tension cleared, and the sun shone again.

Chapter 21

THE TELEVISION WAS tuned to the news for noise. A half-full bottle of Chardonnay sat on the coffee table, which Michaela set down once she refreshed her glass. Michaela's long legs stretched out on the sofa, and the laptop sat on her lap. She gazed at the screen with a self-satisfied face.

Toni's deposit into Michaela's account exceeded her expectations significantly. Michaela hadn't imagined Bianca to be such a generous boss. If Toni's bi-monthly payment reflected that amount, it would do Michaela fine—for now. Toni could access much more once she was married, and Michaela aimed to tap into that wealth.

Michaela set the laptop on the cushion beside her, picked up the cigarette pack on the end table, and rose from the sofa. Her toned body was sheathed in a lavender silk dress that left little to the imagination. Her tanned legs were bare, her nails manicured and painted pale pink. Gold, a recent gift from Sheldon for their memorable weekend, dangled from her ears and long, thin neck. Michaela's golden hair flowed loose around an expertly painted face. Michaela was expecting Sheldon for a quick roll between the sheets before he headed home to his frigid wife.

Michaela's line of expertise was pleasing a man, and she meant not to disappoint. Taking care of Sheldon's needs was par for the course when living in his apartment, drinking his wine, and getting the generous allowance he provided her. Sheldon dashing off minutes afterwards to go home to his wife was no consequence to Michaela. Michaela enjoyed her alone time too much to sacrifice it to babysit a grown-ass man. Win-win.

Michaela stepped out on the balcony. It was a warm day, a little past six in the evening, and men and women in professional attire clocked out for the day and spilled out of office buildings. The streets were crowded with traffic, and sidewalks overflowed with people heading home while others set out for the nearest bar to drink the day's stress. Some headed to local restaurants to enjoy a good meal and entertainment afterward. The smells from the various Chinese, Greek, Italian, and Mediterranean restaurants floated in the air.

Michaela soaked the scenery as she fished a cigarette from the pack and lit it. She could get used to this city again. Michaela's last conversation with Isabella led to threats that made her leave Canada and prevented her from setting foot in Toronto until now.

"I will make sure your parent's friends, co-workers, butcher, barber, bag-boy, hell, anyone who'll listen, come to know what you and your mother are, what you've done. I'll make sure they know what vile, vindictive sociopaths you both are. I will make your life and that of your parents a living hell as you did to me. I will destroy you by any means necessary if you don't leave this country, if you don't leave Bianca and my entire family alone." *Isabella threatened with a fierceness that unhinged Michaela.*

That threat kept Michaela away from Toronto and her parents for decades. But Michaela's parents were now dead, and her inclination to care what people thought about her frayed with age to paper-thin.

Michaela still owned the condominium David Strubb—Isabella's former lawyer and a below-average lover from eons ago—bought for her. Toni knew nothing about the apartment, and Michaela planned to move into it on the premise she recently purchased it to stay close to her loving daughter. Michaela would be sacrificing the rental income on the condo, which had amassed a sizable amount over the years, but she didn't need it anymore. Her baby was marrying rich with access to private jets, worldwide homes, and a bottomless pot of money.

Drawing in smoke, Michaela expelled it in a thin white cloud as she watched the whirling red lights from an ambulance whizz past on Queen Street.

Michaela's plan to get Toni together with Christian had worked better than she anticipated. Michaela knew her daughter well and knew that introducing her to a man close to her age would trigger unexplored emotions in Toni to surface. Michaela understood telling Toni not to fall in love would drive her to do the opposite. The human consciousness was a mechanism of simplicity and easily manipulated.

Michaela's research, or more Sheldon's, told her Toni and Christian shared similar interests. Christian loved children as much as she did. Michaela relied on Christian's close bond with his nieces to give Toni a taste of the family she secretly wished she had.

Toni had never expressed her desire for a family to Michaela, but she knew better. Women who bore children and gave them up lugged a heavy burden that played on their maternal nature. Toni's guilt at giving up her daughter to her lover, Henry Morgan, was a chip that weighed heavily on her mind.

Michaela also knew that giving up the child behind her back and pocketing two hundred and fifty thousand dollars for her benevolent act played havoc on Toni's guilt. Her daughter was too good to commit such duplicitous acts and not feel remorse. She raised her right.

Either way, Toni's vulnerability was there for Michaela to exploit, and she did. The outcome was the blessed union of Toni and Christian Sabatini. Mrs. Toni Sabatini had a nice ring.

Smiling, Michaela congratulated herself on her indisputable, brilliant mind. Taking one last puff of her cigarette, Michaela stubbed it out. Sheldon would arrive in twenty minutes, just enough time to freshen up.

Chapter 22

TONI LOOKED FORWARD to her nightly dinners with Christian with a feeling of discernible thrill. It was their time to spend together after a long workday.

Sat on the stool at the counter, Toni watched Christian in silence, admiring the fit of his jeans that traced his tight butt and the white shirt against his broad shoulders. His hair had a sexily tousled look, and his fashionable stubble had a day's worth of growth that made it look darker.

Christian expertly maneuvered his way around the kitchen as he gathered the ingredients for dinner. Christian chopped garlic with his very large, sharp knife and added it to the two butterflied chicken breasts in the bowl. He then added salt, pepper, and Worcestershire sauce. After mixing all the ingredients well in the bowl, Christian set it aside to marinate.

Christian moved to slice cucumbers, green onion, celery and hand-tore the lettuce. He tossed it with a squeeze of fresh lemon juice and olive oil. Next, Christian turned to the stove and flicked the flame to life to heat the cast iron pan. Adding olive oil and a pat of garlic butter to the hot pan, Christian waited until it fizzled before adding the chicken breasts. Christian sautéed the chicken until golden brown, then added cream, baby spinach, and parmesan, covering it with a lid. It was like watching a finely tuned synchronized dance. Eat your heart out, Gordon Ramsey.

Christian cleared his throat to get Toni's attention when her eyes focused on the Manila envelope from the legal department sitting at the counter's edge. "A penny for your thoughts."

Toni's mind was miles away and distractedly said, "Hmm."

"Are you okay? You seem preoccupied." Christian walked to the refrigerator and selected a bottle of Riesling to pair with the meal.

"I am okay. Just tired and hungry."

Toni's feet were bare, and her hair was caught back into a loose ponytail. She had changed from her professional work look to faded jeans and a see-through rose-coloured blouse tucked at the waist. Christian could see the red lace bra beneath and let his mind roam wildly.

"We need a few more minutes for the chicken to finish cooking. In the meantime, we have wine." Christian walked the bottle and the corkscrew back to where Toni sat.

"Yes, wine, please." Toni drew her knees up to her chest and silently watched him uncork the bottle and pour it into two glasses.

Christian slid the glass in front of Toni when he was done pouring. "I filled it up more than usual. You seem to need it tonight."

Toni picked up the glass of wine, knocked half of it back and felt it loosen her jittery stomach. She held out the glass for a top-up.

Christian topped her glass. "This has to do with the prenup agreement in that envelope, doesn't it?"

Toni's eyes narrowed, and she flicked her eyes to the envelope. Its contents, a simple piece of paper, symbolized so much. It represented mistrust, doubt, and uncertainty. It troubled Toni and nagged at her since the discussion came up. It had given Toni sleepless nights.

Life for Toni was never black and white. It always needed to detour through uncharted territory covered in land mines.

Tearing her gaze from the envelope, Toni shook her head. "No, it has nothing to do with the prenup."

"Of course, it's to do with the prenup. Dinner's on. Let's move to the table." Christian plated chicken and salad and set the plates on the table. "If you don't want to sign it...."

"I do. I will," Toni murmured, eyes focused on the flicker of the candles at the centre of the table.

Christian insisted on candles and a properly set dinner table, whether they ate hamburgers, French fries, or one of his gourmet dishes. It was the way of the civilized world.

Detecting Toni's nervousness and tense shoulders, Christian said, "Well, I had the monthly allowance clause added, but I snuck an increase to the amount because I want you to be financially sound and comfortable. It will be your money to do what you want. To spend as you like."

She thought that was guilt speaking, and Toni blamed herself for it. Toni let her head drop to her folded knees and closed her eyes. After a moment, she opened them. "No, Christian, you must not make special allowances for me. We will change it back to the original amount. I work, and I earn my own money."

Christian watched Toni intently. She had spirit and self-respect and was out to prove she was not the woman she used to be. Once she set her mind, there was no arguing with her. Christian couldn't love or respect Toni more than he already did.

"If that's what you want," Christian said.

"It is, Christian. I do not want special favours. I do not want to take your money or that of your family and have them think I am marrying you for that reason."

Christian put his wine glass down and reached for Toni's hand. "They don't think that, and I know you don't believe it." When Toni didn't respond, Christian went on. "After what Mom and Bianca did for you, for us, I know you know better."

Toni pursed her mouth and pinned her blue eyes on Christian. His apologetic smile and the loving expression on his face arrowed into Toni's heart.

Reassuringly, Toni said, "Please do not let your mind run crazy on you. I need to do this for you and me. I will sign it without hesitation."

"I will let my mind run wild if it causes you to stress out. I don't want you to be upset. You're the only person that matters to me." Christian slid his fingers under Toni's chin and tilted her face up to him. "Look at me and tell me you're not upset over this because if you are, we're not signing this prenup. I don't care what Bianca or my Mom or anyone says."

She lifted her hand and brought it to his cheek. "I care what they think, and it is important to me not to give anyone reason to think I am marrying you for your money but because I am crazy in love with you. You understand that?"

"I do, but you don't need to…."

"I am fine with signing it. I am, really." Toni reached for the envelope. "We will sign the papers now and get it out of the way before dinner gets cold. Tomorrow, you will return it to the legal department to file it or notarize or whatever it is they must do to make it legal as soon as possible."

Chapter 23

THE AIR WAS thick with the smell of brewed coffee as machines dripped espressos and grinders ground beans. The square space was full of sunlight streaming through the long bank of windows. Glass cases displayed muffins, portioned cakes, bagels, and scones. Around the room, on the burgundy walls, were pencilled caricatures of retro singers Frank Sinatra, Aretha Franklin, Dean Martin, and the like. It gave the room a cool vibe.

There was a long line of patrons at the cash register. Some read the menu board on the wall behind the counter while others tapped their feet to Elvis, waiting to place their orders. Chatty teenagers filled the stools at the counter. Well-dressed, self-important men and women tapped on laptops or talked on their phones filled the tables. But the table, two down from her, occupied by the three women, was the one that interested Michaela.

Dressed in lavender running gear and her golden hair held back by a white headband, Michaela sipped her low-fat iced coffee. Impressions were crucial, and presenting herself as a runner while stopping at the coffee shop on the way was essential to her strategy.

Michaela sat at her favourite corner table, focusing intently on Margie, Carole, and Suzanne. Michaela had observed the three of them for days to determine who would best meet her needs.

Suzanne dressed the part of the boss in a navy blue conservative jacket with thin lapels, a teal blouse, and a pencil skirt. Carole and Margie were more casual in dress pants and flowing blouses.

In her shadowing, as Michaela referred to it because stalking was such an unmelodic word, she found Margie, Carole, and Suzanne travelling together everywhere. They were bonded like glue. Michaela surmised the women's close relationship resulted from their shared sexual assault experience at the hands of Bob Klein. A former executive of the Farfalla Corporation, Bob Klein, was fighting sexual harassment charges brought on by Margie, Carole, Suzanne and fifteen other women.

Bob Klein was such a fool, unable to keep his hands to himself and his dick tucked behind a zipped zipper. Men incapable of sexually fulfilling a woman always wanted to share their ineptness. Luckily for Michaela, she only had to endure Bob Klein for a few weeks. Once Bob served his purpose, Michaela sent him packing to fend for himself after broadcasting the women's names on the lawsuit for the world to see.

Sipping on her latte, Michaela stared at the women. Michaela studied, gauged, and assessed which she could turn informer. Michaela needed information on Toni to control her and keep the money flowing to her bank account. Michaela was a youthful woman in her sixties with years ahead of her. She deserved to live those years in comfort.

Michaela could rely on her daughter to do as she was told. Except for the money Toni banked from Henry Klein, Toni always gave all her money to Michaela. Toni did as she was taught.

Now, though, Toni was a woman in love and love made women do crazy, stupid things. Michaela understood that better than anyone. Everything Michaela did, who she was, was because of Antonio Sabatini. He was the only man Michaela loved but could not have because he had only eyes for Isabella—or her money.

A person is never so weak and inclined to cause pain to those closest to them as when they were in love. Toni was no exception. Toni was as deeply in love with Christian as Michaela was with his father and would do whatever was necessary to hold onto him.

Michaela had lied, cheated, and caused hurt for Antonio. Toni would do the same for Christian. Michaela's blood coursed through Toni, and because it did, she knew that regardless of her sacrifices for her daughter, Toni would dedicate all her attention and loyalty to Christian and discard her. That Michaela had raised Toni without help from her useless father and sacrificed was of little consequence to a woman in love.

Michaela seethed at the thought.

Michaela reached into her purse for a cigarette and plugged one into her mouth. She tossed it back into the pack when the server behind the counter pointed to the NO SMOKING sign on the wall.

Taylor Swift's crooning that he was trouble floated over the heads of the customers as people trickled in and out of the cafe.

To be discarded like a used tissue overnight was a hard pill to swallow for Michaela. Michaela reasoned that the least Toni could do was return the favour, support her mother, and give her what she deserved.

Michaela's eyes followed Margie to the counter. Margie was the one who got the drinks and picked up the food for the women. Margie was the one who prepared the coffee for the women, one with cream, one with two sweeteners and skim milk, and another double-double while the women sat at the table and talked. Margie was a good soul, helpful, and subdued.

Michaela, whose eyes had not left Margie over the last few days, decided she made the right decision in befriending her. Margie was a woman who could be easily swayed by others. Margie would perfectly serve her intended role. Margie was the woman who fed Michaela the information about Toni she needed.

"I'll join you once Carole and Suzanne leave for the office," Margie murmured, walking past Michaela's table on her way to hers.

Chapter 24

TONI NEEDED A late afternoon caffeine infusion to fuel her waning energy and rummaged through the cupboards for the coffee pods. Toni had a million things to do, and it was already three in the afternoon.

Unable to locate the pods, coffee tin, or the filters, Toni's frustration amplified. Why couldn't people return things to their rightful spot? Toni launched into an Italian oath-laced rant as she opened and closed cupboard doors and drawers. Nothing. Frustration rose in Toni, and she slammed the drawer shut and set off on a more animated Italian swearing tirade when she caught sight of Margie from the corner of her eye standing at the lunchroom door.

Toni took a calming breath. "I am trying to make coffee."

Margie's face became more downcast, as it often did lately when she ran into Toni.

The air hummed between them. The water spray from the dishwasher as it went through the wash cycle rained solidly in the quiet.

"Do you know where I can find any form of caffeine? Please help me." Toni's voice sounded desperate.

"Bad day?" Margie walked over toward Toni to the length of the cupboards.

Toni nodded. "Very busy. You know how it is with Bianca."

"Yes, Bianca does keep you on your toes."

"I have another three hours of work and need the caffeine boost." Toni moved back several feet to give Margie the distance her cool eyes demanded.

A September sun shone through the window into the empty lunchroom. The smell of Pine-Sol from the floors gleaming clean was strong in the air. The tables were wiped clean, and the chairs were pushed against them.

"Mrs. Lam made her cleaning rounds early today. It was her daughter's first day of school, and she wanted to be there when school let out. Anyway, Mrs. Lam moves the pod bag into the refrigerator after she's wiped the counters clean." Margie's voice was flat as she opened the refrigerator and pointed to the top shelf. "See. There they are. Cappuccino, latte, or espresso?"

"Espresso, please, a double."

Margie picked two espresso pods and walked to the coffee machine. Margie set the first pod into the chamber. After filling the reservoir with water, she put a cup under the spout and pressed the start button.

"You know what to do with the rest."

Margie's voice was artificial and unalive as if forcing herself to speak. Toni hated the feeling of estrangement from Margie, whom she considered a good friend. They had shared laughs and gossip and spent time together enjoying one another's company. Margie, Carole, and Suzanne were Toni's first true friends. Toni was proud to call them friends. Now, because of her mother, everything was different.

"Margie I…."

"I'm only here to help you." Automatically, Margie replaced the pod in the chamber with a fresh one when the machine stopped ticking. "The sweetener is on the table."

Margie filled a glass with water and headed out of the room.

Toni exhaled a breath. "Thank you, Margie," Toni's barely audible voice compelled a tinge of guilt in Margie.

Margie stopped and swirled to face Toni.

"You're welcome, Toni." Margie held the glass of water in both hands and stared into it quietly. After a few minutes of contemplation, Margie lifted her eyes to Toni and said, "I met your mother, Michaela, a few days back," to fill the awkward silence.

Toni blinked, eyes wide in shock. "Where? When? What did she say to you?" The look on Toni's face was one of bewilderment.

Margie told Toni about the coffee shop meeting. "She struck up a conversation with me while we were waiting in line. Through talking, we got on the topic of where I worked, and she mentioned how her daughter also worked for the Farfalla Corporation."

"Yes, I am sure she did," Toni murmured.

"She's charming and stunning and says she misses you. Michaela said you haven't been to see her since she's been in town."

Toni's brows knit, forming a long, shallow line of annoyance between them. "Do not get involved between us, Margie. My mother is my business," Toni said with a sharpness that took Margie aback.

Margie caught her breath. "I'm sorry, Toni. I didn't mean to...."

Toni cut Margie off abruptly. "Then do not, Margie," she shouted.

Toni's mind raced, wondering what her mother wanted with Margie. Because there was no doubt Margie was part of whatever her mother was scheming to do. The spill of damage Margie could unknowingly cause was immeasurable.

Toni's breath exploded in a gasp. "You do not know my mother. You do not know who she is. You are way out of your depth when it comes to Mama." Toni's face was grim.

"Ease up, Toni. A conversation's all it was."

Toni stared at Margie for a long, silent moment.

Toni's emotions were so palpable that Margie felt compelled to walk away.

Chapter 25

PIZZA AND WINE in the comfort of Bianca's living room with the women Toni trusted and could depend on planning her wedding was what tonight was about. Sitting on the sofa to Toni's right was Isabella. Her summer-tanned skin was striking against the orange sundress with thin shoulder straps and a flared skirt. Her chestnut hair was tied into a chignon. She wore muted makeup on her face, which was all she needed.

To Toni's left, Bianca had changed from her sleek white jacket and skirt to work that day into comfortable plum tights with a pink hooded jacket and white running shoes.

Francesca, Aurora, and Mia's images flashed with beaming smiles on the laptop screen as they conducted an animated conversation with Isabella. Francesca, Aurora, and Mia's movements were quick, and they spoke breathlessly. In contrast, Isabella's demeanour was composed and calculated as she offered her flower ideas for the church and venue. Francesca, Aurora, and Mia suggested sprays of white and red calla lilies for the church and roses for the centrepieces. Isabella countered with peach roses and pink carnations in a mauve vase. Each of the women stood firm on their recommendation.

Toni and Bianca watched the animated Italian front, fingers bursting open in the air and heads shaking. Isabella stood firm on her choice. After watching

Francesca, Aurora, and Mia's lively discussion, Isabella mirrored her Italian counterparts' mannerisms, and her voice rose an octave.

"You should say something, Toni. Don't you want orchids?" Bianca bit into Margherita pizza and chased it with Chianti.

Toni followed Bianca's lead and reached for a slice of the homemade pizza Nanny had prepared and plated on a china plate. Like Bianca, Toni wore a flowing shirt and leggings.

"And why would I do that?" Toni leaned back against the sofa's cushion and put her socked feet on the coffee table.

Outside the window, the skyline resembled a Pollock painting as it transitioned from a silver gloss to orange, with strokes of yellow and red. Inside, the living room was brightly lit. Serena, Rosanna, and Romeo were upstairs with Lorenzo, finishing up their homework.

"It's your wedding, and it should be what you want." Bianca licked the tomato sauce clinging to her lips.

"You assume they will listen to the bride." Toni took another bite of pizza. The hot cheese stretched into a long, thin line and dangled from the tip of the pizza to her mouth. Toni wound it around her finger and brought it to her mouth. "Besides this, us getting together is what I enjoy."

Admiring Toni's restraint and laissez-faire attitude, Bianca raised her glass to her. "You, my future sister-in-law, have the patience of a saint. Honestly, I don't know what it is about wedding planning that brings out the Neanderthal in women. I'd stop eating and drink more." Bianca picked up the bottle of wine off the coffee table and topped their glasses.

Toni smiled. "The key is not to pay attention to the noise. Besides, I do not mind someone else planning the entire wedding for me as long as the people I love are there. I do not have the patience or the time for all of this. I would elope and be done with the whole thing."

The women moved on to wedding cake talk. The debate was between a four-tier tiramisu and a five-tier black forest. The Italian front claimed tiramisu was a delicious dessert to be enjoyed with coffee after the planned six-course meal. To their shock and dismay, Isabella informed the Italian front that tiramisu was an outdated dessert. The ensuing argument was loud, and the most animated Bianca and Toni had seen.

Toni shook her head, looking at Bianca helplessly. "Christian and I were expecting thirty people at most, and we are now up to a five-tier cake."

"Well, the list is up to five hundred people." Bianca's comment made Toni wince. "Fifty bucks says Mom will win the wedding cake argument."

"These are three very Italian, strong-willed women against one who is not so Italian anymore and too diplomatic." Toni pointed out. "You are on."

Bianca looked at the three women on the screen, huffing and puffing and then flicked her eyes to a cool and collected Isabella. Age had not mellowed her enthusiasm for negotiating, Bianca thought as she watched her mother make her point with the expertise she'd employed in the boardroom for years. Isabella's eyes were flat, devoid of emotion, a tactic she perfected that gave nothing away to the opponent. Not letting your rival know what you were thinking kept them on the defence.

Watching her mother negotiate, Bianca thought there was something so surreal and admirable. "Mom will win the argument. There's no swaying her when she sets her mind on something."

"Either way, I am not getting in between them. I treasure my hearing and sanity," Toni said with a playful smile.

"Good move." Bianca sipped at her wine and watched Toni over the rim of her glass. "Have you heard from your mother again?"

Toni fell silent, debating whether to tell Bianca of the conversation with Margie and Michaela, who "fortuitously" ran into her. Bianca was the sister Toni never had. Bianca would help Toni navigate through whatever Michaela planned for her next. In this instance, though, Toni opted not to tell Bianca. It was her burden and her fight. Toni had to do it alone.

"While she is getting her money, I will not hear from her," Toni said, averting her eyes from Bianca. The woman could read you to your soul.

"Good. Well, you know I'm here if you need my help." Bianca's face was a mask of sincerity.

Both women turned to the door when it flew open, and Serena, with Romeo barking and chasing after her, ran into the room. Romeo jumped and ran around the room excitedly and chased his tail. Rosanna strode in at a casual saunter.

"Since your tea party, Rosanna has taken her sister under her wing and is spending a lot more time with her." Bianca leaned in to whisper in Toni's ear.

Toni's face filled with smiles. The bond of sisterly love was cherished and shared throughout their lives. "That is good."

"Excuse me, but what have I said about knocking before entering a room?" Bianca scooted over a few inches when Romeo jumped on the sofa between her and Toni, tongue lolling and his tail swishing wildly in excitement.

"Serena, please quiet Romeo down," Isabella said. "Nana is busy over here deciding on a cake for the wedding."

"But, Nana, he's just excited to see everyone. Hi everybody." Serena waved a tiny hand at the video screen.

Serena's chestnut hair was knotted into a braid that hung long behind her, and she wore a pink floral romper with a white T-shirt.

"*Ciao, bella*," the women said in unison, their faces brilliant with smiles.

Serena giggled. "They called me beautiful."

"That is because you are *bella*," Francesca said. "How are you, *amore*?"

"I'm fine. Rosanna and me took Romeo for his potty walk, and we saw a deer. I think it was deer. They looked really big, and they nodded their heads at us, and...." Serena went silent when she lost her thought when Romeo dashed across the sofa to stand beside her. "Romeo says hello." At that, Romeo set off in a barking frenzy.

"Okay, baby, now it's grown-up talk. I need to finish the cake negotiations here." Isabella patted Serena's behind to move her along. "And please take Romeo with you and keep him quiet."

Toni suppressed a smile. "Come sit with me, *amore*. And Romeo, you shush for Nana." Toni signalled Romeo to sit on her lap. "This should keep you quiet."

"And constipated," Bianca said when she watched Toni tear a piece of pizza from her slice and fed it to the dog.

"He has no complaints." Toni and Serena giggled when Romeo devoured the pizza and licked his lips.

"Romeo likes pizza as much as I do," Serena said.

"Now, sit and be quiet for Isabella, Romeo. She is on an important video call," Toni instructed, and the dog looked up with a doggie grin, hopeful to get another pizza taste. "You look very smart today, Rosanna," Toni said low, voiced when Isabella raised the volume on the video call.

"Thank you, Aunt Toni." Rosanna smoothed the front of the short, pleated skirt she wore with a lime-green short-sleeved top. The hairband around her dark hair matched her top, and her cheeks and nose were rosy from the sun. "I'm trying to coordinate my outfits since I'm thinking of becoming a designer like Dad."

"Well, I think you will be very good at it, Rosanna. You have style."

Rosanna's blue eyes danced. "You think so, Aunt Toni."

"I do. Don't you think so, Bianca?" Toni helped Serena settle on the sofa.

Bianca nodded. "I do, too, so much so that Lorenzo will be mentoring you on the weekends. And on the next summer holiday, if you choose to continue to pursue designing, Lorenzo is happy to take you on as an intern. Meaning you will come to the office daily and be paid a salary. Your father wanted to tell you all of this, so when he does, act surprised."

Rosanna's eyes glinted, and her lips spread into a wide smile. The ten-year-old girl surfaced in Rosanna, her cool demeanour melting, and she launched into her mother's arms.

"I want to do it all. And I will act surprised when Daddy tells me. Thank you, Mom. Thank you. Thank you, and I won't change my mind. It's what I want."

Bianca held her daughter tight. It had been long since she last had it, and it felt good. "You can be anything you want, baby. Do anything you want. If you change your mind, that's okay too, do you understand?"

"I do, but I won't. I want to be like Daddy and Nana, and one day, I want to run the company as you do. You don't mind me taking your job, Mom?"

"No, baby, I don't. I'm so proud of you. I'm always very proud of you." A tear spilled over and tracked a line down Bianca's cheek.

"Really, Mom, you are?"

Bianca nodded and hugged her daughter tighter. "I will teach you everything I know so you can take my job. If you like?"

"I'd like that, but first, I want to learn to design. Nana said I should."

"And she'd be right. You need to try your hand at different things. That's how you learn where your strengths and likes lie."

"Did you try designing?" Rosanna asked.

"I did, but I soon found out I didn't inherit the design gene from Mom. I wasn't very good at it."

Rosanna's eyes popped wide. "You weren't."

"No, I wasn't."

Toni sat there watching mother and daughter talk and share the beautiful moment she never experienced with her mother. Toni listened to Bianca's encouragement, never spoken to her by her mother. Deeply touched by the interplay between Rosanna and Bianca and seeing the solidity of their bond, Toni hoped one day to feel pride for her daughter and be as loved as Bianca felt.

Serena bit her lip. "What about me, Auntie Toni? What should I do? I'm too small to do anything."

Toni brushed the stray strands of hair from Serena's face. "You, *amore*, should enjoy yourself with Romeo for now. In a few years, when you are older, you will know what you want to do, and if not, enjoy yourself some more and wait until it feels right for you to decide. Deal?"

"Okay. Are you okay with that, Romeo?" Serena asked, and Romeo answered with a bark. "He's okay with us having fun."

"Good." Toni lightly touched the tip of Serena's nose with her fingertip.

In the background, Isabella said, "A five-tier black forest cake it is, ladies. I will fly you in on the corporate jet for the taste testing and the promised shopping spree at one of my stores."

Chapter 26

THE FEEL OF Christian's capable, experienced mouth electrifying Toni's skin was glorious and doing what he aimed to do, relax her body into pleasure.

"That. Feel. Good," Christian said in between the long, lazy kisses he skimmed over Toni's neck and down her creamy white breasts. She smelled sweet and powdery.

Inhaling deeply and exhaling slowly, she moaned her response.

His lips ripe with a smile of male pride, he filled his mouth with her breast and sucked greedily. Riding on the warmth of his breath and the feel of nipping teeth at her hard nipples, her breath hitched, and her breath exploded in gasps of delight.

Christian's mouth continued to move down her flat belly to the triangle of hair. Her breathing strangled, she arched her body to him when he swallowed her whole. The magnificent hot punch of heat he drove through her body ebbed and flowed in her like stormy ocean waves. Her blood was swimming, and her breaths came in short, raw gasps.

Her pleas became demanding.

Her hands clutched his hair. Her body arched, and her head fell back. Her cries cut through the room's silence as he drove her up—twice.

Christian lifted his naked body above her. Propped on his arms, he looked into her eyes. "How was that?"

Biting on her bottom lip, Toni looked at him. His powerful chest gleamed in the silver light of the bedroom with a light sheen of sweat, and his muscles rippled. "Okay."

Christian cocked his head. "Okay? That's the rating I get." His naked body was inches from her, and she felt his hardness press against her.

Her eyes smiled at him. "I think you are what they call a keeper," she said, and in a swift, sudden movement that took him by surprise, she rolled from beneath him and got on top of him.

"I'm happy to hear." His sapphire blue eyes looked up to meet hers. "The question now is, are you a keeper?"

"I will be happy to prove to you I am," she said, taking possession of him.

Locked together, the wet, hot feel of her was intoxicating. Gripping her hips, he thrust himself deeper and harder inside her.

She moved with him, rose and fell in synchronicity in the choreographed dance that was theirs. In the growing momentum, she hammered the orgasm through him. As he filled her, his grunt was loud, potent, and male. She thought she saw his eyes roll back in his head for a few seconds.

Toni leaned over and kissed Christian on the lips. "So, am I a keeper?"

Christian ran a fingertip down Toni's cheek. "You are, not because of the great sex or because you're a firecracker, exciting and bold, but because I love you and want to share moments like these with you for the rest of my life."

Toni smiled winningly. "I love you too. So, so much."

Naked, they lay quietly curled up against each other. Christian's arm wrapped around Toni while she traced small circles with the tip of her finger on Christian's chest. Both gazed out the window at a darkened morning sky peppered with flashing streaks of lightning as rain fell steadily, drumming against the window.

Toni thought there was no better place to be and no better person to share the moment with.

Sometime later, Christian slid out of bed. Without an ounce of modesty, he stood naked, facing Toni. Christ on a bike! The man was magnificent, Toni thought, eyeing the tall, leanly built body with broad shoulders, muscular arms, tapered waist, and long legs. And he was all hers.

"I'm going to grab a shower. Do you want to join me?" Christian said, reaching into the night table drawer for the glass jar.

Toni was about to accept the invitation when her cell phone rang. Rolling over in bed, she picked up the telephone off the night table. "It is Bianca. I have to get this."

"Okay, but remind her it's Saturday, your day off, and she's not to keep you long on her crises du-jour." Christian held up the bottle in his hand. "It's that coconut oil you like me rubbing on your body in the shower."

Toni gave him a sunny smile. "It is the coconut oil you like rubbing over my body."

"Potato, potahto," Christian said with a grin as he walked toward the bathroom.

"I will not be long." Toni pushed off the bed and, reaching for Christian's T-shirt on the floor, slid it on.

Toni walked toward the window. It was a blustery day, the first of many as summer slid into fall. The rain beating against the windowpane washed down, blended to make one long streak of water, and hazed the view of the gardens, pool, and the roll of land beyond it.

Taking a deep breath, she answered the ringing phone. "What do you want? I told you not to call me at home on the weekend," Tony spoke softly to keep Christian from hearing her.

"Is that any way to speak to me?" Michaela spoke with a sweetness that she did not possess.

When Toni heard the shower water running in the bathroom, she said, "What do you want, Mama?"

"I'd like to know why you'd ask Christian to draw up a prenup document and why you would sign it."

"How do you know about that? That is confidential information. I want to know who in the company you have talked into giving you information." Toni demanded, and when the silence lingered, she said, "It is Margie who you so happen to run into. Isn't it? She has been giving you internal company information."

Michaela ignored the comment. "So it's true you asked for it. Have I not taught you anything?"

"Yes, you have taught me a lot, and that is why I asked Christian for the prenup." Toni's tone was defiant.

"You stupid, stupid girl."

"No, Mama, it is a smart move. I will never have access to Christian's money, nor will you."

"Goddamn it, Toni, what's the point of marrying rich?" Temper, lava-hot, poured out of Michaela.

"I love Christian, not his money. I love him for the understanding, selfless, loving man he is," Toni said, staring out the window at the wall of rain battering it.

Michaela laughed cynically. "Pfft, love. What do you know about love?"

"Nothing from you. What I know about love I have learned from my father, my new family, my fiancé, and his family." That would hit home, Toni thought.

A sudden chill settled over the telephone line. The silence was deafening, and Toni waited it out.

Michaela wasn't good at handling rejection, and Toni ascertained the expression on her mother's face at the implication of her words. Toni imagined her mother's rising anxiety as her mind whirled with all manner of resentment and anger. Toni pictured Michaela's face contorting like a rabid dog's at the thought of Joe Smith and Isabella Farfalla's family supplanting her. It pleased Toni.

"As I said, I know much differently now. I know what true love is and what it is to be loved, and I will protect my family and friends at any cost. That means protecting them from you, Mama, and whatever nonsense you have planned to get at their money."

Michaela didn't hear the usual desperation in Toni's voice or the frail woman she was accustomed to. At the end of the line, the woman speaking wasn't the weak girl she knew. Toni sounded confident, strong, and fearless.

Unnerved, Michaela said, "Well, I have your father's contact information now and...."

Toni promptly cut Michaela off. "And nothing, Mama. You will do nothing and not call him with any demands. You will have to settle for the amount of money I give you, which is my paycheck, money that *I* earn. I have no more to give you."

"You're marrying a billionaire," Michaela snapped with the ferocity of a roaring lion, and still, Toni heard the faint sound of desperation in her mother's voice.

"It is not my money to give, and you will get none."

Michaela's distress at the loss of control of her daughter robbed her of speech. The heavy silence drifted for a while.

"You forget that if you don't give me what I want, I will tell your newfound family all there is to know about you," Michaela said after some time. "If you refuse, you'll force my hand, and I'll tell your father that I will tell Christian everything unless I get one million dollars deposited into my account by the end of the week. I doubt Joe would be keen on unsettling his baby girl's life and damaging her prospects with such a great catch after neglecting you all of his life."

That hit Toni and got deep into the bottom of her psyche. Toni went silent.

"One million dollars, Toni, or I reveal all, understood?"

"Please do not do this, Mama." Toni's voice was small and soft. "Please, Mama." Toni's plea went unheard when Michaela hung up.

"Your mother's been bothering you?" Christian's unexpected voice caught Toni off guard, and she swirled to see him standing by the bed, a white towel wrapped low around his hips.

"How long have you been there?"

"Long enough."

"You like eavesdropping on my conversations?" Toni snapped out of a combination of guilt and embarrassment.

Damn her mother for trying to destroy the only semblance of a decent life she's had.

"I didn't mean to. You took a long time, so I came to rescue you from Bianca, and I hear you pleading with your mother to leave you alone." Toni's face reddened. "How long has she been in contact with you?" Christian took a few steps toward Toni but stopped when she took an equal number of steps back.

"A few weeks." Toni averted her face from Christian's piercing eyes.

"What does she want?" Christian's voice punched like a fist. "What does she want, Toni?" Christian repeated when she remained silent.

"Money, but I am handling it, Christian." Toni's voice sounded strangled.

"How much is she asking?"

"It does not matter because I am not giving her a cent. I am taking care of this." Toni stared back at him with defiant eyes.

Christian walked toward Toni. This time, she didn't back away. "I don't want you to take care of it yourself, Toni. We're supposed to be a team, a couple. We're supposed to work things out together." Christian chained his arms around Toni. "I want you to share your life, the good and the bad, with me. We're in this together, Toni."

Toni pulled away from Christian's embrace. "I told you I am taking care of this," she barked at him.

"All right. Fine," Christian relented. There was no point arguing with Toni once she got that resilient, bold look in her eyes.

Toni paused and stared out the tall window sheathed in a waterfall of rainwater. For a brief moment, all that could be heard was the rhythmic sound of rain and the distant rumble of thunder. Toni remained that way for some time, thinking and debating whether to tell him everything.

Truth shall set you free, the silent voice in her head said. Toni thought that was the biggest load of bullshit she'd heard.

Telling Christian about Angelica wouldn't benefit anyone, least of all her daughter. Secrets were meant to be contained because once out, it was a matter of time before they wound their way to the ears it was meant to be kept from. Not telling Christian would be a secret at the heart of their relationship, and one day, he would come to resent her for keeping it from him.

Toni remained motionless, contemplating her ruin.

Bombarding Christian with the never-ending mistakes that, until recently, were the fabric of her life of depravity should be done gradually. As resilient and resolute human beings were, the human psyche couldn't absorb so much unpleasantness in quick doses.

After some time, Toni turned to Christian, silently sitting at the edge of the bed, his hair curled wet, his eyes fixed on her. Toni walked to Christian and sat beside him at the edge of the bed.

"Do you trust me, Christian?" Toni looked at him with solemn, conceding eyes.

"Completely, and you know you can tell anything and everything."

"And I will when the time is right. Okay?"

"Okay." Christian put his arms around Toni, and she fell on him.

Chapter 27

JOE LOOKED AT his telephone screen. It read Unknown Caller. His back stiffened, and his shoulders tensed.

Over the years, Joe had expected the call. Joe avoided answering the telephone for the longest time, fearing it would be her at the end of the line.

It took years of therapy and all of Joe's strength to shake the heavy feeling of dread bearing down on him and eating a hole in his stomach day in and day. The stress that became a part of Joe's life with Michaela took time to cast off. The aftermath of the anxiety Joe endured, the peptic ulcer, took months to repair. Only by the grace of God and Francesca's help was Joe able to dig himself out of the void that was his life with Michaela.

Now, with a singular telephone call, it was all back. Years of therapy were unravelling. The feeling of drowning in deep, murky waters without seeing the surface in sight took over. There was no worse feeling than losing control over yourself and life, which was how Joe felt.

Joe stood frozen in place, deciding whether to answer the telephone.

Joe thought he'd prepared and psyched up for this moment. He was wrong. He reached for the nonexistent elastic band on his wrist to tug and remembered he'd freed himself from it years ago.

Joe breathed in deeply through his nose and exhaled through his mouth.

When Joe regained control, he closed the door to the study behind him. "Hello."

"Hello, Joe," Michaela said.

After all these years, hearing Michaela's voice, the sinking sensation in the pit of his stomach struck hard. Joe's throat went tight and his mouth dry. The anger Joe tucked away long ago surfaced inside him again in one fell swoop. Joe reached for the bottle of scotch on his desk. Uncapping it, he drank straight from the bottle.

"What do you want?" Temper snapped in Joe's voice.

Always the drama queen, Michaela thought. "I'm fine. How are you, my dear ex-husband? It's been too long since we last spoke."

As if nothing ever happened, Joe thought, hearing her indifferent tone. He spent years on a therapist's couch scrutinizing the design of his life, dissecting it to rework it from what it was. Yet, to Michaela, it was as if nothing happened.

Joe reached for a cigarette, lit it, and inhaled deeply. Joe let out smoke in a quick stream. Joe did that a couple of more times to regain control.

"What do you want, Michaela?" Joe's tone was sharp and cold.

"So that's how it's going to be. We were an item back in the day. So very much in love. Remember those days, Joe?"

Joe heard the amusement in Michaela's voice and thought that nothing had changed. Everything had always been a game to Michaela.

"I'm a very busy man. I don't have time for your bullshit. Say what you called for."

Detached interest, Michaela thought. It was never like that with Joe. Michaela's thoughts wandered to their sex life. No lover she had since Joe matched his stamina or thirst for adventure in the bedroom. Michaela's smile widened as she recalled Joe's untamed libido and the fantastic sex they shared anytime and anywhere.

Only Joe knew how to satisfy Michaela's needs. As a teenager, Joe was well versed in the physiology of a woman's body, and Joe knew Michaela's well.

Michaela could feel Joe's hands and mouth on her then. Christ! The things he could do with his mouth.

There were still times when, late at night, Michaela slipped her fingers under her lace panties, and Joe, not Antonio, was the man of her conjured fantasies. Hearing Joe's voice now, the familiar heat struck Michaela, and she let her fingers wander. She was deliciously wet and wasn't surprised. Joe always had that effect on her.

"I've missed you, Joe. Do you remember the fun we used to have?"

The corrosive nausea rose in Joe at the idea he'd once shared her bed. "I'm only going to say it one last time before I hang up. What do you want?"

Michaela listened to Joe's warm, vibrant voice and inched her fingers farther into the moist heat. "All I want is a bit of spending money."

"What leads you to the misguided belief that I'd give you any money?" Joe lit another cigarette with the flaming tip of the smoked one.

Michaela's finger ran along the silky dampness and made the liquid warmth spread. "Because if you don't, I will tell Christian your little girl's secret."

"Toni's told him and me everything, every vile thing you forced her to do."

The fury simmering in Joe's voice brought back flashes of their erotic trysts. Michaela thought of the number of times Joe took her in the men's bathroom of Antonio's café.

"Not everything. This secret is so much worse that our daughter couldn't tell the man she loves, or you, for that matter." It wouldn't be long now. Michaela stroked faster. "One million dollars into my bank account by the end of the week is all I ask," she said between muted ragged breaths.

Joe puffed hard on the cigarette. "You fucking, horrible excuse of a human being, how do you live with yourself?"

Michaela felt her self-control slipping. "By the end of the week, Joe or I tell Christian and let the chips fall where they may." Michaela's breath hitched, and she let her head fall back onto the back of the sofa and closed her eyes. "But they won't hear anything if I get the money by the end of the week."

In the ensuing silence, Michaela filled her head with images of Joe doing whatever he wanted to her while her hands were cuffed to their four-poster bed.

"Even if I believe you, what's to say you won't return for more money and keep your mouth shut?"

Joe caved. Michaela's lips stretched out in a smile. There was the weak excuse of a man she knew.

"I promise you not to say a word or make any other demands."

"Your word is worth shit." Joe's voice was steel, and by Christ, she loved it.

The orgasm struck fast and hard, and Michaela let out an orgasmic moan and cried Joe's name, as he liked.

Joe slammed the phone on the desk.

Michaela opened her eyes and smoothed her hair into place. "Incredible as always, Joe."

Michaela needed a cup of green tea.

Chapter 28

MICHAELA TURNED THE ignition off on the canary-yellow Corvette she had leased after Sheldon refused to let her use his car. Michaela wasn't sure what triggered Sheldon's sudden one-eighty-degree turn, but to hell with Sheldon. Today was payday, and Michaela did not need him anymore.

Stepping out of the car, Michaela gave the stunning home the once over. The glow of delight on her face was swift.

The last time Michaela was here was in darkness, and she could not take it all in as she did now under the bright sunshine glowing in a blue sky. Michaela's eyes perused the professionally manicured gardens hemming the house and the stretch of green land dotted with willows, maples, and firs.

It was impressive, and now, it belonged to her little girl and, by extension, to her, Michaela reasoned.

Stifling her merriment and replacing it with a blank face, Michaela smoothed the floral silk dress that clung to her curves. Michaela straightened the wide-brim sun hat, tucked the Ferragamo envelope clutch under her arm and made her way to the front door.

"Can I help you?" Christian said when he opened the door to the beautiful woman with the pouty red-plum-painted lips.

Michaela stared at Christian. He looked nothing like your stereotypical accountant.

Christian's eyes were as blue as the sea, and his face was handsome, rugged, and familiar. Christian was, after all, the spitting image of his father, Antonio.

"You are a gorgeous specimen." Michaela's eyes twinkled brightly. "You look just like your father."

"And you are?" Christian paused for a moment when a sudden ominous feeling trickled through him. Belated recognition flashed in Christian's eyes, and his expression hardened. "You're not welcome here." Christian slammed the door in Michaela's face when Toni appeared in the foyer.

"Let her in, Christian," Toni said. "She is here to see me. Please."

Christian opened the door, and Michaela's gaze settled on her daughter. Toni's jeans were designer and expensive. The silk turquoise shirt she wore was Farfalla branded, worth hundreds of dollars. Toni's hair spilled around an unpainted face. As pretty as her daughter was, she had learned little from her, Michaela determined. A woman had to put in more effort than wearing designer labels to keep her man's interest, or she would find herself sitting across from him at an oval boardroom table with her lawyer.

"Why? Why would I let her into our home?" Christian gasped.

Michaela's eyes sparkled with a smile. The way Christian's nostrils flared, and the fierce, icy gleam of his pale blue eyes flashed with anger made him unmistakably like his father.

"We have business to discuss," Toni said.

Christian gaped at Toni in shock. "I don't want her in our home, and you shouldn't either."

"I have tea in the living room." Toni pointed to the first door on the right and watched Michaela saunter toward it. "Give us a minute, Christian."

Christian's mouth tightened. "What are you doing, Toni?"

"I promised to explain everything to you when the time came. The time has come," Toni said, and, closing the front door, ushered Christian to the living room.

Michaela sat on the sofa, her long legs crossed and her purse and hat at her side. The diamonds at her ears glittered when they caught a quick strike of the sunlight streaming through the window.

"You have a lovely home, Christian. Yes. Stunning indeed." Michaela scanned the valuable artwork hanging around the room she failed to see on her last visit. "It makes a mama proud to see her little girl well provided for and by such a handsome man. You really do look so much like your father."

Christian stopped abruptly. "Don't think I'm here to make friends with you because that's the farthest...."

Toni interrupted Christian to prevent the incoming verbal flare-up that would not help her cause. "Please sit down, Christian."

"Yes, please sit, Christian." Michaela patted her hand on the seat next to her, and Christian walked to the furthest chair from her and sat. "Do I scare you, Christian?"

Toni telegraphed a look that told him not to take the bait, and Christian pursed his lips. "Here you go, Mama. Cream and sugar as you like it."

Michaela took the offered cup. "Thank you, baby. I have a dinner appointment in an hour, so let's get to the business at hand."

"Yes, let us." Toni walked to Christian and sat on the arm of his chair.

Michaela stared at Christian and Toni. They made a beautiful couple. She commended herself on choosing well for her daughter. "You're going to give Isabella and me beautiful grandchildren."

"You lost the right to breathe the same air as Mom, let alone say her name." Christian's eyes were hard as stone.

"I like the fire in him. I hope he brings that passion to the bedroom. Does he, Toni?" Michaela's tone was one of pure amusement.

Toni clamped her hand on Christian's arm when he opened his mouth to speak. "Let us get down to business, Mama."

"Let's, my darling daughter. Since Christian's here, I assume he knows about the million-dollar payout."

Christian looked up at Toni, his eyes aghast. "You're giving her a million dollars?"

"I have been giving her my paycheques," Toni admitted.

A frown line deepened between Christian's eyebrows. "How's that possible when your paycheques have been deposited into our joint account?"

Michaela's eyes lit up. "You have a joint bank account?"

"We do, but you are not getting any more money. You are not getting any more paycheques, let alone one million dollars. You are not getting any money from Papa, who I believe you called to blackmail." Toni's voice was subdued and calm.

Christian looked from Toni to Michaela. "You're trying to blackmail Toni and the man whose life you terrorized for years?"

"Terrorize is such an unmusical word, and your interpretation. I was a helpless woman living with a psychopath. Besides, I had to take drastic measures because of your wife-to-be." Michaela casually stretched her arms across the back of the sofa. "I warned your fiancée I'd call Joe if she didn't come through for me. I figured today's meeting was her changing her mind when I proved my warning to call her father if she didn't come through with the payment wasn't an idle threat."

Pursing his lips, Christian looked at Michaela thoughtfully, wondering what made a psychopath because it was clear that's what she was. That Toni was a well-adjusted, good person with a mother like Michaela was a miracle. Many don't survive the effects of a dysfunctional parent, especially one as flawed as Michaela.

"An idle threat?" Christian's face was muddled with puzzlement.

"I see you haven't told your husband everything." Michaela stretched the last word out for emphasis. "Secrets in a relationship are the death of it."

Toni met Michaela's steadfast gaze. "No, I haven't told Christian everything. Not yet. I need you to listen to this first." Toni opened the laptop on the coffee table and cued it up to play the recording.

They listened to the recording of Michaela firmly threatening Toni, stating that she would spill the secret unless she received one million dollars in her account.

"There's more." Toni cued up the next recording.

They heard Michaela threatening Joe to reveal Toni's secret to Christian unless he deposited one million dollars into her account.

"So." Michaela casually sipped at her tea.

Christian looked at Toni with questioning eyes. "What haven't you told me, Toni? I thought you'd told me everything. What could be worse than what she's made you do?"

"I will tell you everything. I promise, but first, I must take care of her." Toni tilted her chin toward Michaela. "I will turn over these recordings to my lawyer, who will follow up with the police. As it happens, extorting money through blackmail is a criminal offence. Life imprisonment is the maximum penalty for an extortion crime, which is the threat of revealing embarrassing information unless money is paid to purchase silence. That is what Henry Morgan, my lawyer, said."

Michaela dropped the tea saucer and cup on the coffee table with a thump. Whether because of the mention of Henry Morgan's name or the threat of imprisonment made no difference to Toni.

"Your bribe to Papa will be used to file charges against you, ensuring you remain out of Italy and away from him and his family. My family. You see, Mama, you taught me well," Toni exclaimed.

Michaela's imperious attitude evaporated like steam on a cold day, and she fell into a momentary silence, reflecting on Toni's words.

The silence hung heavy in the room until Michaela sprang up from her seat unpredictably, picked up the laptop, and tossed it across the room with brute force.

"Hey, that's a brand new laptop." Christian started to push off his chair to pick it up when Toni clamped a firm hand on his shoulder. Christian remained seated.

"Toss it around all you want, Mama. The recordings are uploaded onto the cloud for safekeeping and will remain there forever to use when I want. Modern technology is such a wonderful thing." Toni calmly picked up the laptop off the floor and set it on the console table away from Michaela. "If you come anywhere close to my family, friends, coworkers, or Christian, I will not hesitate to have Henry Morgan follow through. He will pursue charges against you." When Toni stopped speaking, she watched Bianca and Margie enter the living room.

Michaela stared at Bianca. Tall, beautiful, in a very expensive Farfalla coral suit, her bright blue eyes glared at Michaela. Bianca was the spitting image of her mother. Margie looked inconsequential next to Bianca. No surprise. Margie came from women who settled for what life handed them, thought Michaela.

"What the fuck are they doing here," Michaela snapped like a Pitbull.

"You know Bianca and Margie." Toni looked at Michaela, whose eyes flashed like two hot flares at her daughter. "They helped set my plan up." Now, Toni looked at Christian. "Bianca doubled my salary so I could pay Mama half and deposit my usual paycheque into our account so as not to raise suspicion while I did what I had to."

Michaela's anger became more resilient. She was quivering.

"Margie and I have worked together since I found out Mama approached her and attempted to manipulate her into giving her information on me, the company, and you, Christian. She told me what Mama asked for, and I fed her the information to take back to her. Margie has been a great friend." Toni reached for Margie's hand.

Margie tightly squeezed Toni's hand. "I found out through Ming on my venting rant that Michaela, not Toni, was the person circulating the women's names suing Bob Klein for sexual harassment for something as abject as money. When I did, I felt shame and regret for being such a bad friend, and I decided to tell Toni about my recent association with her mother. Instead of hating me, when she calmed down," Margie said with a smile, "Toni was understanding and forgiving. When Toni asked me to help feed information to her mother, I didn't hesitate to agree. Toni coached me on what to say to Michaela and the information to pass on. I also told Carole and Suzanne everything. We're all friends again."

"And they will remain friends without intrusion from you, Michaela." Isabella entered the room looking matriarchal in white pants and a cerulean blouse. Her chestnut hair flowed in waves around her face with few lines. She wore sapphires at her ears and a blinding wedding ring with a diamond worth more than Michaela cared to admit. "I thought we were done with your intrusion into our lives long ago, but here we are."

Michaela's returned Isabella's stare. "Only because you're stealing my daughter from under me like you stole everything else in my life."

Isabella poured herself a cup of tea, added sugar and cream, and stirred. "You're still under the diluted assumption I stole Antonio from you when all you were to him was a pesky customer he couldn't swat away like an annoying bug."

Toni's eyes widened, and her brows raised high when it suddenly became apparent she was Antonio's namesake. How had she not seen it before?

"Don't listen to her. She's always been a vindictive, lying bitch." Michaela said, her voice rising, hardening. "How could you do this to me? I'm family. Blood."

Christian gauged the temperature in the room, which rose twenty degrees. It was not a surprise when Mama Bear was in the room. Strong, spirited women like his mother tended to rile up the room. Christian sat back to enjoy the show.

"No, you're not family or blood relation. You and I know it, but that's a conversation for another day." If the sudden shock of Isabella's disclosure surprised Michaela, it didn't register on her face. "And no, Michaela, unlike you, I'm not vindictive. I'm stating fact. That Antonio and I have been married for over four decades and are still very much in love speaks volumes." Isabella sipped at her tea.

"Not vindictive, you say. Then why introduce my daughter to the abusive father I shielded her from, who stalked and assaulted you several times?" Michaela barked.

No one but Margie, whose mouth twisted into a nonverbal Jesus, reacted to Michaela's remark.

"Stalking and assaults, which you instigated." Isabella lowered herself onto the sofa facing Michaela and artfully crossed her legs.

"Careful with your accusations, Isabella. You have no proof of that unless your fallback is that Joe was in love with you and wouldn't dare hurt the woman of his obsession." Michaela looked around at the shocked faces in the room. "You heard right," Michaela growled.

Now, everyone but Margie reacted with shock to Michaela's comment. Margie wished she knew who Joe was.

Dazed by the revelation, Bianca's knees buckled, and she fell on the sofa. "Is this true, Mom? Joe was in love with you?" Though Bianca's voice was calm, Isabella could see the angst in her eyes.

"Joe's been in love with your mother for as long as I can remember." Michaela turned to Toni with a feigned wounded expression on her face. "Your father never loved me, baby. Do you know how defeated and unloved I felt? Do you know what it's like to devote your life to a man you love and never return that love? No matter what I did, I couldn't break through emotions fiercely cemented in him for another woman."

Bianca stared at Isabella. "Were you in love with Joe?"

Isabella saw something so sad resonating in her daughter's eyes. Isabella imagined every thought rolling in Bianca's mind led to questions of Joe and the DNA report's veracity. Isabella expected Bianca to grapple with doubts about the DNA result, which she assured established that Joe was not her father. Bianca refused to acknowledge anyone as her father except Antonio and chose not to read the report. But Isabella read the report and afterward shredded filing it away as ancient history.

Bianca had trusted Isabella's assurances that she was not Joe's daughter all these years. But that was in doubt now. When uncertainty is cast, the mind is easily swayed to doubt everything you were told or believed. Bianca wondered whether Isabella purposely shredded the report to prevent her from seeing the results. Maybe Joe was her father. Bianca regretted using the last strand of Joe's hair, which Isabella had kept locked up in her safe for years, to determine Toni's relationship with Joe rather than establish hers.

The tears started down Bianca's face.

Isabella slid her fingers under her daughter's chin and tilted her face until their eyes met. "I was never in love with anyone but your father. Your father was my first and only love. He was the first man in my life. I didn't know Joe was in love with me until he found me in Milan when he came to warn me about Michaela and asked for my forgiveness. Joe told me he would never hurt me because he'd been in love with me since high school. Everything that came about, the stalking and assaults, did because I never saw how he felt for me and because Michaela took advantage of Joe's deepest vulnerability. Now, she's trying to manipulate you, Christian, and Toni into believing something that doesn't exist. Don't allow her to fracture us as she intends to do."

Toni's eyes swivelled to Bianca. "Isabella is right. My mother is a master manipulator, which is what she is doing now. Papa loved Isabella. That is true, but he never told her, and Isabella never knew how he felt and did not reciprocate his feelings. Papa told me Isabella's head was full of your father, and there was no changing it. Papa told me he only came to understand Isabella's devotion to Antonio when he met Francesca and fell head over heels in love with her. Only then did Papa understand what it was to love wholly and fully and be equally loved unconditionally."

"They've brainwashed you with all this love bullshit." Temper whipped colour into Michaela's face at the apparent betrayal by her daughter.

"No, Mama, I have not been brainwashed. My new family, my friends," Toni reached for Christian's hand and held tighter to Margie's standing next to her, "has taught me what unconditional love, loyalty, and friendship are. I will say this for the last time, Mama. You will leave my new family, Papa, friends, and me alone. You are never to contact any of us again. If you contact anyone in my life or me, I will turn the tapes over to Henry Morgan. If I know Henry, he will not fail to do what is necessary to keep you locked up for a long time."

When Michaela started to open her mouth, Toni held up a silencing hand.

"There is nothing you can say of shock value to change my mind. I, however, have much to say to you. Sheldon Tanner has been warned not to help you again, or he will lose much of his lucrative business. Friends of Isabella who will not hesitate to dump him on her say so. Guess which option Sheldon chose? Two, you will sell your downtown condominium." Toni watched Michaela's stunned eyes stare back at her. "Yes, Mama, I have known about it all along. You will sell it and never set foot in this country again. I want you out of my life permanently. Take heed of what I say, Mama, because I mean every word." Toni's eyes were unyielding, and her voice firm.

Something inside Toni had calcified, and her resolve to remove Michaela from her life was compelling. In Toni's eyes, Michaela saw a kind of steely resignation she never saw before, and she blamed Isabella and Bianca. Those two manipulative bitches brainwashed her daughter and turned her against her.

Fury simmering, Michaela swung her head and aimed glaring eyes that would have set everyone in the room on fire if she could. "To hell with all of you," Michaela grunted between clenched teeth and stormed out of the room.

Christian grinned. Christ, he loved the women in his life.

Part III

The End

Love is the ultimate liberator. It can heal our deepest wounds and free us from the shackles that restrain us.

—M.L. Lexi

Epilogue

TONI REMAINED SILENT as, from the living room window, she watched Michaela's Corvette speed off down the driveway and fade in the distance. Her mother was gone from her life.

Toni remained rooted in the spot for a long while, her blue eyes staring out the living room window. Her sombre eyes trailed the pair of blue jays that winged from tree to tree over the rich colour of the gardens, catching the last sunlight strikes before evening fell.

Although Toni propelled her mother's abrupt departure, and as much as she knew it was the best thing for her mental health, the guilt was all-consuming. The woman was her mother.

You can choose your friends, but not your family.

Today, however, Toni did choose. She chose her new family over a toxic relationship with the woman who gave her life. Toni chose Christian, Bianca, Lorenzo, the girls, and Romeo. Toni chose Isabella and Antonio, Joe and Francesca, their vocal, animated brood, Margie and Suzanne and Carole over Michaela.

It was the best decision Toni had ever made.

Toni was about to embark on a new life with a man who unconditionally loved her and the people who embraced her despite her past life. Her psychotic mother would come nowhere near them. Toni would make sure of that. Toni wouldn't allow her mother's toxicity to permeate their lives as she had hers.

Toni was prepared to protect her new family no matter what it took.

Holding onto that thought, Toni turned her head, but for Christian, she faced an empty room. "Where did everyone go?"

"They wanted to give you space. They're in the kitchen making coffee, and if I know Mom, lacing it with tons of Irish whiskey."

"Perfect. That is what I need right now," Toni said.

"Mom thought so. She always knows what's right."

"She does."

Christian walked to Toni and took her in his arms. "Are you okay? That was a lot to deal with."

"I am." Toni pillowed her head on Christian's chest and breathed in his scent. She felt a measure of comfort come over her. "I will be."

"I'm sorry you had to deal with all this alone."

"I am sorry I brought this to your doorstep, into your family's life. I'm sorry I lied to you," Toni whispered against his chest.

"You did nothing wrong. Do you understand?" Christian said, and Toni nodded. "I understand you needed to do what you did today on your own, but from here on, we're a team. I don't want you carrying the burden of anything that troubles you and weighs you down alone. I'm here to support you and help lighten the load. Is that understood?"

Toni nodded as her mind rolled over her life before Christian.

So many mistakes and regrets were woven into the fabric of Toni's life. Yet Christian accepted them—as her past. Christian represented the calmness and stability Toni had never had in her life. Above all else, Christian made Toni feel safe. Christian would protect her. He would keep her whole and nurture the woman she wanted to be. Because of Christian, Toni would never lead the life of degradation she lived before him.

Toni would have the children she always wanted, and they would be a part of both of them with values they could be proud of. Christian finally offered a glimpse of the normal life she had always longed for. Because of Christian, she would become Toni Sabatini, a respectable woman with a worthy name.

"Understood," Toni said and hesitated for a moment. "I have something to tell you, Christian."

"I expect you do, and whatever it is, we'll deal with it together, but not today. You've had enough to process for the day. Okay?" Toni nodded. There was a moment of silence before Christian said, "Let's get married tomorrow."

Toni looked up and met Christian's eyes. They held an expression in them that tugged at Toni. She understood the proposal to marry sooner than later was to fill the void she felt from her mother's departure and give her a sense of family.

Christian brushed Toni's hair back and away from her face and looked deep into the blue eyes. "You didn't want a big wedding anyway, so let's do this."

"Do what?" Isabella walked into the living room with Bianca and Margie, carrying trays topped with tall glasses of Irish coffee adorned with swirls of whipped cream alongside glasses of milk, croissants, and chocolate chip cookies.

"Get married now, tomorrow or next week at the latest. I don't want to wait two more months for Toni and me to marry."

Isabella's all-encompassing look took in everything. Christian was her sensitive child, and Isabella's razor-sharp mind quickly discerned his sudden urgency was for Toni's sake.

Isabella looked at Toni. "What do you say, Toni? Do you want to get married now?"

Toni's stunned surprise dissipated, and she looked into Christian's eyes. "I want what Christian wants."

"Mom, we still have so much planning to do." Bianca pointed out. "Toni's dress, the bridesmaids, or any of the dresses for that matter, isn't close to ready."

Isabella raised a hand to silence Bianca. "If that's what Christian and Toni want, it's what we'll do." Isabella walked up to Toni and took her hands in hers. "But, honey, I'd love you to wear a white dress and walk down the aisle. I want you to watch Serena, Rosanna, and Emilia toss red rose petals leading to the altar. It symbolizes fertility, you know, and I want to make sure it sticks because you'll give me beautiful grandchildren." A slow smile slid across Isabella's face. "And Romeo wants to strut down the aisle in his bowtie with your wedding rings. It's not for us I want to do any of this for. I want those memories for you." Isabella touched Toni's face with the tenderness and affection of a mother. Toni's eyes glittered with moisture.

In her thirty-six years, Toni had never heard her mother speak to her with such selflessness, love, and kindness. Feigned hints of affection were what her mother was about.

"So, how about a compromise? Next weekend, we'll get you two married in a civil ceremony and a reception at my house. That'll give us time to fly Joe, his family, and Mama and Dad in from Italy because I know they wouldn't dare miss your wedding. As we've been planning, we'll have the church wedding on Christmas day. What do the two of you say?"

Christian pivoted his face to Toni. "I'm good with whatever you want."

"That sounds wonderful, Isabella, absolutely wonderful." Toni wrapped Isabella in a fierce hug. "Thank you for everything."

"You're welcome, honey. Now, Bianca, order pizza, Chinese, and whatever other food you think will feed the expected army of people. Christian, you fetch a few bottles of wine. Margie set the table. Toni will help you. Chop, chop, people, we need to have dinner on the table quickly. We have a party to plan." Isabella ordered, and everyone knew better than not to heed her instructions.

"We're having a party?" Serena ran into the living room, with Romeo chasing after her. She wore a purple top, pink leggings, and matching sneakers. "Hear that, everyone, we're having a party. I like parties, and so does Romeo."

Rosanna followed, and Lorenzo was close behind as the front doorbell rang.

"I'll get it. That's probably Carole and Suzanne." Margie announced, dashing out of the living room.

"I hope you don't mind, but we invited the clan and your friends. Antonio should be here soon," Isabella said to Toni.

The cacophony of animated conversation rising over the clinking glasses and the laughter reverberating in the room as Rosanna chased Serena, who chased Romeo around the sofa with his tail swishing in excitement, lent a feeling of family. The family Toni could now rely on. This was the safe harbour in a storm, a world of vivid colours, laughter, music, love, and possibility.

"No. No, I don't mind at all." Toni looked around the crowded living room, feeling complete and triumphant.

Her mother was no longer inside her, making everything hurt, making her a broken woman. Toni Trevi was dead.

She was Toni Sabatini, the invincible woman.

Sneak peek at M.L. Lexi's new novel

THE PERSEVERING WOMAN

Prologue

Spring 2007

THE PROCESSION OF cars following the black hearse into St. Paul's Presbyterian Cemetery was thirty long. Slowly, the cars made their way through the cemetery to Mrs. Emily Johnstone's final resting place. A few minutes in, the hearse stopped before the mausoleum Isabella had built for Mrs. Johnstone's last resting place.

The mausoleum, constructed of white marble, stood tall amongst the headstones jutting from the snow-covered ground. Above the entrance door, a hand-carved angel strummed a gold lyre. On opposite sides of the door, colourful orchids speared from tall white urns. It was a grand structure, but Isabella Farfalla believed it was what Mrs. Johnstone deserved.

Mrs. Johnstone was much more to Isabella than the bank manager, who decades ago gave a young, naïve girl the opportunity of a lifetime. Emily Johnstone was a friend and mentor. Because of Emily Johnstone, Isabella owned and managed the worldwide renowned billion-dollar Isabella Farfalla Fashion empire.

Because of Mrs. Johnstone, the fashion-conscious sought Isabella's designer clothes, handbags, shoes, accessories, and perfumes. Mrs. Johnstone's foresight had made it possible for celebrities, the elite, and royalty to want to be seen in Isabella Farfalla's original design. Isabella's elegant, graceful designs had walked down the red carpet, appeared on various theatrical stages, and worn at galas, Hollywood award shows, first ladies, and royalty. Isabella's designs and gold butterfly logo were as recognizable as Gucci's interlocked "G" s and Chanel's bold interlaced "C" s.

As much as Isabella's husband, Antonio Sabatini, and Sal Mesi, her biological father—who appeared in her life decades later—ultimately had a hand in her success, Emily Johnstone believed in Isabella enough to approve the loan that helped launch her company.

Opening the car door, Isabella stepped out. The air was crisp, and cooler air prevailed, but the drizzle of snow that fell melted under the late morning's bright sun.

Filling her lungs with air, Isabella raised the collar of her coat. Her long, glossy mink hair was a dark contrast against the cream-coloured mohair coat. She wore black knee-high boots with a high spiked heel and pointed toes. Isabella's brown, red-rimmed hazel eyes were shaded behind dark Farfalla sunglasses. At sixty-five, her olive skin remained mainly untouched by the many hardships she'd faced. Maybe more than most had dealt with, but perseverance made Isabella come out a survivor in the end.

Closed doors led to open ones was Isabella's philosophy. That creed helped Isabella overcome homelessness after her father's death at the unfair young age of forty-one left her with mounting bills. Isabella's philosophy helped her survive bankruptcy, betrayal, blackmail, and the stalker who ultimately traumatized her and stole her dignity and life.

For twenty-one difficult years, Isabella doubted her daughter's origin, and the doubt remained at the heart of her marriage for as long. Keeping the secret internalized and keeping it from Antonio, her husband, was the hardest thing Isabella had done.

When the truth emerged twenty-one years into their marriage, Antonio declined to read the DNA report and unquestioningly accepted Bianca as his daughter. Antonio stuck by Isabella then, and four decades later, he was still by her side, his love for her as ardent as ever.

Closing the car door behind him, Antonio reached for Isabella's hand and held it tight. Isabella looked over at him. He'd aged like a fine Italian wine. Hovering on his seventieth birthday, he was still as handsome as when she met him.

Antonio's hair, dashingly grayed at the temples, crowned the handsome face with the sea-blue eyes she fell in love with. He wore a navy tweed coat over a black silk suit with a white shirt, burgundy tie, and brown Mesi derby shoes. Isabella smiled. As striking as he looked, Antonio was never comfortable out of his customary jeans and a cotton shirt with the sleeves rolled to the elbows.

After Antonio successfully launched The Café franchise across Canada, Isabella tried to talk him out of the cotton shirt and jeans and into a more professional look. Isabella failed miserably and just as well because she did not mind admiring the six-three-frame fit in those snug jeans.

"Are you all right?" Antonio reached for Isabella's hand and held it tightly.

"I already miss her," Isabella said softly. "It feels as if it's the end of an era."

"Yes, but in all fairness, and no disrespect to Emily, she was ninety-two," said Antonio.

"Dad's ninety-three, and Mama's not far behind." Isabella watched Bianca and Lorenzo attempt to corral their daughters, Rosanna, ten and Serena, seven, from running off when they exited their car with little success.

"Youthful energy," Antonio sighed with a smile. "Your father and mother, amore, much like Emily, are a force to be reckoned with. For God's sake, Emily outlived three husbands. As for your parents, they still have enough energy to keep up with those two girls and all their great-grandchildren."

"Are you going to leave the girls lying in the snow?" Isabella said to her daughter on her approach. Bianca wore a gray coat, tapered black pants and laced-up ankle boots.

"They'll get tired soon enough and join us." Bianca shouldered her handbag, brushed the chestnut hair that tumbled in waves around her face and straightened the sunglasses, shading the blue eyes so much like her father's. "Lorenzo will deal with them. He has the patience of a sloth."

We do marry our parents, Isabella thought, watching Lorenzo patiently handle the girl as Antonio would.

"But never mind the girls, Mom. Are you all right? You weren't doing well at the church."

Isabella brought her hand to Bianca's cheek. "I'm fine, honey. Cold, but fine."

Bianca watched her father's arm tighten around her mother's waist in a circle of comfort and warmth. Here was love, Bianca thought. Her father would move mountains for her mother if she asked him. Bianca hoped she and Lorenzo would be as in love and devoted to one another after decades of marriage as her parents were.

"She was such a lovely woman—tough as nails but lovely. She taught me loads. I will miss Mrs. Johnstone, and the girls will miss their second Nana." Bianca turned to watch her girls lay down on the snow to make snow angels while Lorenzo watched on. "Christ, I have to put a stop to this. They're getting their coats wet and dirty."

Isabella caught Bianca's arm before she turned to go. "Leave them, honey. Emily wouldn't mind one bit. If anything, she'd encourage the laughter and fun they're having, as her family does. See what I mean?"

Bianca, Antonio, and Isabella watched Mrs. Johnstone's gaggle of great-great-grandchildren, encouraged by their parents, lay down next to Rosanna and Serena with them watching on.

Over the giggles and laughter of the children making snow angels, Christian walked up and did precisely what Isabella predicted of her thirty-eight-year-old son. He lay next to Rosanna and Serena in the snow.

Bianca's slash of dark eyebrows rose. "He needs to get himself a wife."

Isabella nodded. "Yes, he does." Isabella looked at Antonio then. His eyes were bright and smiling. "You need to speak to him."

"Yeah. Sure. I will." Antonio agreed when Isabella narrowed her eyes. "Your parents are here," he said to change the conversation.

Isabella waved Salvatore and Maria over. "Let's get to it. Bianca, honey, round the troops and have everyone head to the mausoleum. Emily was a stickler for punctuality in life, and we're not about to start to disappoint her now."

THERE WERE SO MANY PEOPLE THERE. It was easy for an outsider to blend into the group, but she stayed well behind. Some of those in attendance flew in from around the world to attend Emily Johnstone's funeral. Unlike what she'd been told, Emily Johnstone wasn't a hated woman. Emily Johnstone was very much loved.

Blue Eyes scanned the group. Isabella and her clan, the Sabatinis and the Mesis, were there. It was rumoured Isabella paid fifty thousand dollars to build the mausoleum where the stiff was to be buried.

Blue Eyes hated rich people. Blue Eyes' fingers lightly tapped the tree as if striking piano keys to deal with the mounting resentment eating her insides.

Blue Eyes saw the famous runway model Kat LeBlanc, now Kat LeBlanc-Mesi, who, thanks to Isabella, went from working as a receptionist for Emily Johnstone to the runway. From there, it was a matter of time before Kat got her hooks into Isabella's bastard brother, Carlo Mesi, and became one of the wealthiest women in Europe.

Kat risked her perfect modelling figure to give Carlo the twin sons to carry his legacy. It was a paltry gesture for what she got in return, thought Blue Eyes.

Blue Eyes saw the old man, Salvatore Mesi, Isabella's biological father, who had started the company Carlo had taken over. His wife Maria, Isabella's biological mother, whom Salvatore left knocked up, stood by him. The only reason Blue Eyes could think of for the old woman to take Salvatore back after abandoning her when she was pregnant with Isabella had to be for his money. What respectable woman takes back a man who disappears overnight and reappears decades later?

Blue Eyes flicked her attention to Christian when he approached the hunky Lorenzo Romano. Lorenzo wasn't just an excellent designer, but he was a whole lot of gorgeous. Blue Eyes was sure she could fulfill his wildest fantasies in bed better than his pretentious, haughty wife Bianca could. Blue Eyes let her mind wander for fifteen seconds before forcing herself to focus. Christian was the man she'd flown across an ocean to meet, not Lorenzo.

The long, dark curls, the broad shoulders, the fashionable stubble, and those blue eyes had her swooning. Christian looked better in person than in the photographs she had seen on tabloid covers and pages. She could see why he was labelled the most desirable bachelor.

Sexy good looks were a plus, but that didn't interest her as much as his bank account. Christian Sabatini was worth millions, and that very much interested her.

Coming Soon

The Complete Woman
The Conflicted Woman
The Spiteful Woman
The Tortured Woman

The Relentless Woman Duology

The Relentless Woman
The Vindictive Women

The Unbreakable Woman Trilogy

The Unbreakable Woman
The Brave Woman
The Valiant Woman

Contact us

Email us at mllexiauthor@gmail.com to receive emails whenever M.L. Lexi publishes a new book. There is no charge or obligation and your information will remain confidential.

Visit us at www.mllexi.com to read excerpts of upcoming releases.

www.ingramcontent.com/pod-product-compliance
Lightning Source LLC
Chambersburg PA
CBHW022121170626
46808CB00002B/805